# MOOSE
## Chase

SIOBHAN ROWDEN was born in Scotland and brought up in England. She has a degree in English and has worked as a holiday rep in Corfu, at Disney World in Florida and for a production company in London. *The Curse of the Bogle's Beard* was her first novel followed by *Revenge of the Ballybogs*. She lives in Brighton with her husband and children. She doesn't like blue cheese.

www.siobhanrowden.com

@SiobhanRowden

# WILD
# MOOSE
## Chase

Siobhan Rowden

SCHOLASTIC

First published in the UK in 2014 by Scholastic Children's Books
An imprint of Scholastic Ltd
Euston House, 24 Eversholt Street
London, NW1 1DB, UK
Registered office: Westfield Road, Southam, Warwickshire, CV47 0RA
SCHOLASTIC and associated logos are trademarks and/or registered trademarks
of Scholastic Inc.

Text copyright © Siobhan Rowden, 2014

The right of Siobhan Rowden to be identified as the author of this work
has been asserted by her.

ISBN 978 1407 13873 2

A CIP catalogue record for this book is available
from the British Library.

Printed by CPI Group (UK) Ltd, Croydon, CR0 4YY
Papers used by Scholastic Children's Books are made
from wood grown in sustainable forests.

1 3 5 7 9 10 8 6 4 2

www.scholastic.co.uk

To Pete, for keeping me warm
inside and out.

# The Curds of Whey Farm

Camilla and Bert Curd were twins. Not identical twins. They hated being compared and were quick to point out that Cam's long hair was fairer and Bert's eyes were greener. To keep them happy, their grandpa called them *very-similar-but-completely-different-twins*. Bert was convinced that he was slightly taller, a lot faster and generally much better at everything. Cam was equally certain that she was the fast one, at least three millimetres taller and far superior in every way.

However, much to their annoyance, there were

certain times when they did look exactly the same. It was usually when they were scared or worried. One half of their mouth would pull down and the other half would go up in a strange diagonal line.

They were both wearing this expression as they raced across the top of a steep gorge in the pouring rain. A flash of lightning lit up the grey evening sky, revealing a vertical drop on one side, a herd of cattle on the other and a shrieking old woman behind.

The cattle scattered as they leapt over a rough wooden gate away from the cliff edge and towards a ramshackle farmhouse in the distance. Cam tripped and rolled over on the wet grass, narrowly missing a huge cowpat. She scrambled to her feet, glancing nervously behind her. The old woman had stopped at the fence. She was still shrieking but the wind carried her voice away.

"Bert, wait for me!" panted Cam, sprinting after her brother. "She's right behind us."

"No way!" shouted Bert over his shoulder. "I think she's given up, and anyway – a race is still a race!"

They sped past the cows and vaulted a five-bar gate leading towards the ancient farmhouse. One wall bowed dangerously out and the whole building looked like it was about to collapse. A heap of crumpled bricks stood where the garden wall should have been. Wild flowers and weeds poked through the rubble. Bert tore up the path towards the crooked wooden porch.

"I win!" he cried.

Cam came scrambling after him. "That's not fair! I tripped over!"

"Loser! Loser!" chanted Bert, falling against the front door.

To his surprise, the thick wooden door creaked open under his weight and sent him tumbling inside. Cam almost laughed but stopped suddenly as a large figure emerged from the dark hallway. It was cloaked from head to foot in white and breathing heavily. Two enormous gloved hands reached out and hauled Bert to his feet. The twins looked up into the rasping masked face.

"Hi, Gramps," they said together.

The figure pulled off the mask, revealing a crinkled old man.

"Phew, it's hot in that beard net," he puffed. "Shut the front door and take off those muddy coats before you contaminate my cheesemaking overalls. I've just come from the dairy."

Cam nervously checked outside before pushing the old door shut.

"Is she coming?" whispered Bert, wriggling out of his wet jacket.

Cam shook her head and hung her coat next to Bert's on a large cow horn sticking out of the wall.

"What are you whispering about?" asked Gramps, stepping out of his overalls.

"Nothing," said Bert.

Gramps studied the two *very-similar-but-completely-different* faces in front of him. Droplets of water still sat on their grubby noses, magnifying the odd freckle.

"What were you up to out there in this weather?" he asked. "You weren't racing again, were you? These competitions of yours always lead to trouble."

4

"It was just a running race," said Bert, "and I won."

"You cheated!" shouted Cam. "I fell over and you didn't stop to help me."

"That's not cheating! It's not my fault you have butter-toes. You're always tripping over your own feet."

"I do not have butter-toes!" cried Cam. "I couldn't see where I was going. The storm clouds came and it got really dark. We ended up somewhere we shouldn't have been."

"You better not have been climbing the cliff," grumbled Gramps, marching through to a cosy living room where a huge fire blazed. "Cheddar Gorge is nearly one hundred and forty metres high. You mustn't go in the caves either. Some of them are prone to flooding, and if you got lost. . ."

The twins followed him into the warm room.

"We weren't in the caves or climbing the cliff," said Cam, slumping into a deep sofa. "Stop fussing, Gramps."

The old man's eyes clouded as he stood with his

back to the fire. He began jingling the change in his pockets, which he always did when he was cross or upset.

"Stop fussing?" he repeated. "It was a stupid racing competition that killed your parents ten years ago and I will not let the same thing happen to you!"

The twins glanced guiltily at each other. Although they couldn't remember their mum and dad, they still felt sad, especially when their beloved Gramps welled up at the memory.

"I promised to take care of you and you're not making it easy for me," he continued. "Why does everything have to be a competition? Who's the fastest, who's the tallest, who's going first, who's going last! It's getting out of control. One of you is going to get seriously hurt – or worse!"

He wearily crossed the room and slowly sank on to the sofa between the twins.

"You should appreciate each other," he sniffed. "Stop competing and look at what you have. You are 'the incredible Curd twins', full of potential. Bert, you have your father's special way with animals – a very rare gift. If you were as nice to your sister as you are to our cows then we'd all be a lot happier. Cam, you're as bright as a button, and you've got your mother's caring nature. It would be nice if you could extend that towards your brother. Your parents would have been so proud."

They all sat for a moment staring at the fire in front of them. Eventually Cam put her arm around her grandpa.

"Sorry, Gramps," she whispered.

Bert did the same on the other side. "Yeah, me too," he said. "I'm *really* sorry."

There was a mild scuffle of arms behind Gramps' neck.

"I'm really *really* sorry," murmured Cam, as she pushed Bert out of the way.

"Not as sorry as me," said Bert in a loud whisper, shoving his sister.

Gramps sighed again and shook his head. "Just no more competitions – OK?" he said. "Anyway, if you weren't climbing the cliffs or exploring the caves, where were you?"

Bert pulled a face. "When we were racing, we might have accidently on purpose ran across Primula Mold's farm and jumped over a few goats. It was the quickest way home."

Gramps' eyebrows knotted together in a deep frown. "Primula Mold?" he muttered. "I've told you to keep away from that monstrous old crow next door. Stay off her land! She will be furious! She'll have your guts for garters, your ears for ornaments, your toes for tinsel, your—"

He stopped talking as a large cowbell hanging above the doorway jerked from side to side, dinging loudly. Gramps eyes swivelled from the bell to the twins.

"That's her!" wailed Bert, diving under the sofa. "She can't have my ears or my toes. I like my toes! Hide!"

# 2

## Primula Mold

Gramps stood up and pulled Bert out from under the sofa by his ankles.

"Go and answer the front door," he said. "This is your own fault – both of you."

The twins crept along the hall. Bert pushed Cam in front of him.

"This is your chance to come first," he mumbled.

"Age before beauty," muttered Cam, trying to pull him in front of her.

"I'm only two and a half minutes older!" cried Bert. "And it was your idea to run across

Primula Mold's land."

"Wasn't."

"Was."

"Wasn't."

They fell against the big front door as the bell rang again. Gramps stood behind them, his hands on his hips.

"Stop fighting and open that door!" he said.

They both pulled the heavy door ajar. A flash of lightning lit up a thin old woman. Her blue-rinsed hair was pulled back into a tight bun, stretching the skin across her hollow face. The twins shrank back behind Gramps. They couldn't bring themselves to look at their neighbour. She produced blue cheese, and Gramps said never to trust anyone who injected their cheese with mould.

Primula Mold's bulging black eyes swivelled angrily from the twins to their grandpa. A large wet basset hound emerged from behind her, his long ears dragging on the muddy ground.

"Good evening, Miss Mold," sniffed Gramps. "What brings you out on a night like this?"

"Those children are out of control," she barked, stabbing a bony finger at them. "They were trespassing on my land today, worrying my goats."

"We were just running home," murmured Cam.

"Screeching you were!" shrieked Miss Mold. "Screeching like a pirate's parrot and scaring my animals. If it happens again I'll set Fungus on you."

They all looked down at the wet dog. A pair of large brown eyes stared back at them from beneath a wrinkled brow.

"Fungus wouldn't hurt a fly," said Gramps. "But the twins would like to apologize."

He looked pointedly down at Cam and Bert.

"S-sorry," they said together.

"And in future," Gramps continued, "I'll make sure they walk around your land and keep the noise down. Now, if that's all? Goodbye."

He began to close the door but Miss Mold stuck her large muddy boot in the doorway.

"No, it's not all," she snapped. "I have some other very important business to discuss with you."

Gramps sighed and peered out again.

"Concerning the World Cheese Fair," added Miss Mold.

Gramps looked up sharply. "Well, in that case, you had better come in," he said, opening the door wider.

The twins pressed their backs against the hall wall as Miss Mold barged straight past them into the living room.

"I can't believe you let her in," hissed Bert.

"I had no choice," whispered Gramps. "Tomorrow is the biggest day in the cheese calendar and if she's got some news, I want to hear it."

"The World Cheese Fair," said Cam, brightening up. "I'd forgotten it was coming. Will there still be lots of delicious food and fairground rides and animal shows and hot air balloons and—"

"Competitions?" finished Bert.

"Yes, all of that," said Gramps. "Come on; let's hear what she has to say."

They followed Primula Mold into the lounge. She was wandering around their living room slowly examining the faded furniture and chipped ornaments. Her damp green overalls clung to her skinny frame. Bert thought she looked like a giant stick insect. She had neglected to take off her mucky boots, which were now making dirty footprints on the hearthrug. Dangling from a long chain around her neck was her "lucky Stilton". It was a round cheese the size of a saucer, given to her twenty-five years ago by her father on his deathbed. The pungent smell of old cheese began to fill the room. Fungus waddled over to them and Bert bent down to stroke him.

"Are you prepared for tomorrow, Mr Curd?" asked Miss Mold.

"I've just been putting the finishing touches to my prize cheese," said Gramps.

"You shouldn't have bothered," she said, smiling smugly. "I'm fully expecting to win 'Best Cheese in Show' for the fourth year running."

Gramps bristled. Miss Mold rubbed her lucky Stilton.

"My past wins have really boosted international sales, allowing me to upgrade my dairy," she continued, "and I need to expand. Mold Farm has been catapulted into the twenty-first century, whereas Whey Farm. . ."

She trailed off and looked around the tired room, sighing theatrically.

"We prefer the traditional methods here," stated Gramps.

"How quaint. But rumour has it you've fallen on hard times."

The twins frowned and looked across at Gramps. He slowly lowered his hands into his pockets and began jingling furiously.

"I heard on the cheese-and-grapevine," continued Miss Mold, "that if things don't improve, you might have to sell up."

A loud crash of thunder shook the farmhouse, rattling Gramps' ornamental cheese graters, which were proudly displayed on the mantelpiece. Cam and Bert gasped in dismay. Fungus, who was resting his head on Bert's lap, let out a low howl.

"Who told you that?" bellowed Gramps. "Whey Farm has belonged to the Curd Family for generations. It's one of the oldest dairy farms in the country."

He walked proudly round the room, straightening his ornamental cheese graters and patting the chimney breast.

"Four hundred years ago. King Charles the First purchased the finest cheese from our very own farm. Back then, the caves of Cheddar Gorge were used for maturing the cheeses. And that wasn't our only royal connection. Queen Victoria was very partial to a bit of cheddar too. Things may have been slow lately, but if I win 'Best Cheese in Show' at the World Cheese Fair then everything will be fine. It will bring our cheddar back into the international market where it belongs."

"And if you don't win. . .?" asked Miss Mold.

Gramps didn't reply, but the jingling coming from his pockets was unbearable.

"We've been neighbours for a long time," she said. "I would be willing to buy your land when the time comes."

"The time will never come!" cried Gramps. "Now,

if you'll excuse me, I really haven't got time for this conversation. I have to prepare for tomorrow." He gestured towards the door.

"I see," said Miss Mold. "Then I suppose you won't have time to hear about another royal connection."

"What? Who?" asked Gramps.

"Apparently, we are to expect a special visitor at the fair tomorrow. Royalty of the highest order – the big cheese – the top dog."

"Is a corgi coming?" asked Bert hopefully.

"No, you cheese-brain! It's the Queen!"

The twins leapt up in excitement and Fungus began barking. Gramps' cheeks flushed red, making his whiskers glow.

"She's obviously heard about Queen Victoria's love of our cheddar," he cried.

Primula Mold shook her head. "I'm afraid it's well known that the blue bloods prefer the blue cheeses," she said.

"Rubbish!" spluttered Gramps.

"And besides," Miss Mold continued,

"appare..., the [...]

competiti...

The twi... [...]

and stared at ... Mo...

"Competiti..." they [...]

"That's all I k... ... [...]

the hall. "I suppos... ... [...]

We must all be on... [...]

you can control tho... [...]

Come, Fungus. We ha... ... had dinner

yet and my mildewed m... ...oni is in the oven. I'll

let myself out."

The small dog toddled after his mistress.

"Bye, Fungus," called Bert.

A cloud of leaves blew in as the front door

opened, then slammed shut.

"Well, well," said Gramps, sitting down. "The

Queen at the World Cheese Fair, eh? What do you

think of that, kids?"

"I can't believe it!" cried Bert.

"It's fantastic," agreed Cam, "but what about the

farm? Was Miss Mold telling the truth?"

at. Everything will be
g to be *extra* special. We're
Queen."

ns were excited. Very excited. A
tion set by the Queen! Surely Gramps
uldn't say no to that.

# The World Cheese Fair

The World Cheese Fair was held every September at the highest point of Cheddar Gorge. Three slender fingers of rock, known as The Pinnacles, towered hundreds of feet above the winding road below. Huge marquees were erected along the clifftop, following the horseshoe bend and curving round to make an enormous circle of colour and noise. Cam and Bert ran ahead of Gramps, who was carefully carrying his prize cheese. There was no sign of the storm that had sprung up the night before, but every speck of dust had been blown from the sky and the twins could see for miles over the hills. Several hot air balloons rose from the fair, giant orbs of colour splashed against the brilliant blue sky. The twins could just catch faint wafts of music coming from a colossal Ferris wheel soaring above the marquees.

"I'm so excited," said Bert. "Feel my heart. It's racing."

Cam reached over and placed her hand on his chest. "It's not as fast as mine," she said. "Mine's faster."

"No it's not."

"'tis."

"'s not,

"You're saying 'snot'."

"*You're* saying 'snot'."

"Come on," said Gramps. "Let's see if we can get through today without an argument, shall we?"

They wound their way through the food stalls on the outskirts of the fair. One was selling oddly shaped vegetables. There was a five-fingered carrot, a potato that looked just like a famous footballer, a cow-shaped cucumber and a string bean that reminded Bert of Primula Mold. They lingered at a colourful cheesy-sweet stall with jars full of halloumi humbugs, mozzarella marshmallows, feta fizz bombs, cheddar dib dabs and various cheesy chewing gums. Gramps said he would buy them a bag each if they got through the day without fighting. They passed a bizarre pickle stall, selling cheddar chutneys, pickled cheese on toast, and cheesy-toe shavings. The large old lady behind the counter belched loudly as they peered at the cheesy-toe shavings, and they moved on quickly. They marched through a whole street of cheese tents, waving and greeting the various stallholders.

"Morning, Lester," shouted Gramps to a red-headed man with a kiosk full of orange cheeses. "How's the wife and baby Belle?"

"Fine, thanks, Mr Curd," said the man. "Let's have a look at that prize cheese of yours."

Gramps wandered over and proudly presented his cheese.

"Gramps, can we go and explore?" asked Bert. "We can meet you in the Show Tent later."

"Go on then," said Gramps, handing them some money. "And be nice to each other."

The twins skipped off. They passed an enclosure full of tiny goats. Bert stopped to stroke one. It rolled over on its back and kicked its legs in the air as Bert tickled its tummy.

"Mind my pygmies!" cried a little man.

"Just saying hello," said Bert. "C'mon, Cam, let's find the rides and roundabouts."

They followed the strains of music coming from the fairground rides and came across an enormous merry-go-round. But instead of horses bobbing up and down, it was giant wedges of cheese.

"ROLL UP, ROLL UP, FOR THE MERRY-GO-CHEESE," shouted the man in charge.

"Bagsy the mature cheddar," yelled Bert.

"I want that one," cried Cam.

But Bert had already barged past and clambered up on to the large wedge. Cam folded her arms in a huff.

"No need to sulk," said the man. "There's a mild cheddar over there, or a Stilton on the other side."

Cam reluctantly climbed on to the mild cheddar.

"There's no way I'm going on a Stilton," she fumed.

A small child was crying as her father carried her up on to the ride.

"But I don't want to ride a cheese," she wailed.

Her father looked concerned. "Not even Wensleydale?" he asked.

When the crying child had been removed and the ride was full, the roundabout began to turn.

Cam was still mad because her cheddar was slightly behind Bert's and it felt like he was in the lead.

"Hurry up, Cam," shouted a gloating Bert from in front.

The ride got faster.

"Actually, this is the front," said Cam. "You're a long way behind at the back of the roundabout."

A large boy was next to her, precariously perched on a piece of Parmesan.

"I didn't know circles had fronts and backs," he said.

"They do when you're in a race," she explained.

Cam began to feel dizzy as they gathered speed. She looked across to Bert's wedge. It was empty.

"Are you looking for him?" asked Parmesan boy, pointing to the other side of the merry-go-cheese.

Bert had climbed off his cheddar and was jumping from wedge to wedge. The other children were screaming and clinging to their cheeses as he leapt on to their slices and slowly made his way round the ride.

"I'm catching you up," he yelled, the wind streaming through his hair.

Cam stood up, clinging tightly to the long pole that pierced her cheese like a giant cocktail stick.

"Oh no you don't," she muttered, diving on to the empty mature cheddar in front. She almost toppled right off the other side but managed to cling on.

"Butter-toes!" laughed Bert.

Cam ignored him and heaved herself up again. There was a shout from behind.

"Get off my cheese!" yelled Parmesan boy.

24

Cam looked behind her. Bert had joined Parmesan boy on his tiny wedge. The man in charge looked up just as Bert made a final jump back on to his own cheese, which Cam now clung to.

"Oi!" he shouted, pulling on the brakes. "One child, one cheese!"

The twins were still wrestling to get in front when the merry-go-cheese came to a halt.

"What do you think you're playing at?" said the man. "If you'd fallen from that ride when it was—"

He stopped as a huge object drifted above them, blocking the sun and casting an enormous dark shadow.

They all looked up. A hot air balloon twice the size of the others and shaped like a gigantic crown floated above the fair. A golden basket dangled underneath.

"Look!" cried Cam. "Look who it is!"

Bert frowned.

"Someone with a really massive head?" he asked.

"No, you nincompoop-a-scoop!" laughed Cam. "It's the Queen! She's here!"

# 4

## The Queen

The twins squeezed their way through the crowds to where the Crown Balloon was about to land. It settled in a large enclosure in the middle of the fair to the strains of "God Save the Queen", performed by a military orchestra. Several attendants grabbed the ropes hanging from the sides of the huge golden basket and pulled the balloon gently in, securing it tightly to the ground. A red carpet was rolled out, leading from the basket to a nearby stage with a large podium positioned in the middle. The twins spotted Gramps' white hair sprouting up at the front of the crowd. They ducked down and crawled through everyone's legs until they reached him.

"Hello, Gramps," they said, popping up either side of him.

"You're just in time," he said. "Here she comes. Isn't she glorious?"

The twins watched as the Queen slowly made her way along the red carpet and up on to the stage. She was dressed in a long purple coat with matching shoes. Her grey curly hair poked out from under a lilac-brimmed hat. Bert was disappointed that she wasn't wearing a crown, but guessed it must be quite chilly riding in a hot air balloon. A small dog stayed close to her heels. She was followed by four trumpeting guardsmen and a thin man with a huge curly moustache, wearing a flat triangular hat. The Queen smiled and waved at the cheering crowd. Gramps bowed low as she stood up to the podium and waited for the fanfare and the cheering to die down.

"My lords, ladies and cheesemongers," she announced. "My family and I are, and always have been, great cheese enthusiasts."

The crowd clapped eagerly.

"My son is patron of the Specialist Cheesemakers Association and my corgi"– she smiled down at the small dog by her feet –"is patron of the Easy Cheesy Doggy Treats Society. Both of whom are represented here today."

Two men in dog outfits with "Easy Cheesy" embroidered on their ears cheered loudly from the back of the crowd. The Queen carried on speaking.

"I have come here today with a challenge for the world's finest cheesemakers."

Bert glanced at Cam. "This is it," he whispered. "The competition."

"I will be hosting a state banquet here in Cheddar Gorge in precisely six days' time," said the Queen. "And the French president himself, Monsieur Grand-Fromage, will be our guest of honour."

There was more cheering and lots of "bravo"s coming from the Brie and Camembert tents.

"Monsieur Grand-Fromage is a cheese connoisseur," she said, "and knows his fondues from his fon-don'ts."

"What's a *con-o-sir*?" whispered Bert.

"Someone who knows lots about something," said Cam. "Unlike you."

"However," continued the Queen, "there is one dairy delight that neither the French president nor I have ever tasted."

She paused and looked around at the eager crowd.

"A cheese like no other; a cheese that some believe has mystical powers and others think impossible to make. A cheese so rare that I will bestow the title of lord or lady on anyone who can present it to me in time for the state banquet. I want. . ."

The audience held their breath.

". . .moose cheese!"

A shockwave seemed to ripple through the crowd before erupting in loud cries of disbelief.

"Impossible!" gasped Gramps.

"Why?" asked Cam, looking round at the excited crowd. "What's so special about moose cheese?"

"It's the holy grail of cheeses," whispered Gramps. "Nobody has successfully made one in hundreds of years. The ingredients are extremely rare and scattered across the world. But tales of its exotic flavour have been passed down the generations. The taste is indescribable. There are many ancient myths and stories detailing its magical qualities. Some say that one mouthful can bring you a lifetime of health; others believe that it brings wealth. Maybe a whole cheese will bring both. Who knows? Apparently it glows like a light bulb."

"It must be hard to milk a mouse," said Bert.

"Not mouse cheese!" cried Cam. "*Moose* cheese!"

"Milking a moose may be even harder," whispered Gramps. "But listen, Her Majesty hasn't finished yet."

Beside the Queen, the thin man with the large curly moustache was holding his hands up for silence. Cam noticed that his yellow hat looked like a large wedge of cheese. Everybody slowly calmed down.

"The Royal Cheesemaker, Mr Gordon Zola,

will now hand out leaflets detailing the rules and regulations for the competition," said the Queen, nodding towards the man in the hat. "I realize that it will require much more than just cheesemaking skills to produce such a dairy masterpiece. Some of my very own serving staff have tried and failed to obtain the ingredients despite travelling halfway across the world, from Siberia to Mongolia and beyond."

There were more cries of astonishment from the crowd.

"As many of you are aware, some men have paid the ultimate price in their quest to produce moose cheese." She briefly glanced across at the Royal Cheesemaker, who was now handing out golden leaflets to the excited crowd.

"And that is why," she continued, "the maker of such a culinary treasure will not only be honoured but will also receive a cash prize of five hundred thousand pounds!"

A collective gasp rose from the audience.

"Any further questions you may have will be

answered by Mr Zola, who will oversee proceedings and report directly back to me."

Mr Zola took his cheese hat off and bowed to the Queen before handing Gramps a leaflet and moving on.

"What does it say? What does it say?" cried Bert, trying to get a look at the shining notepaper.

Gramps held it up for them all to see.

Her Majesty the Queen is pleased to announce

# THE GREAT MOOSE CHEESE CHASE

Contestants have six days to obtain the ingredients listed below and produce a traditional moose cheese in time for the State Banquet with special guest Monsieur Grand-Fromage of France.

The winner will receive £500,000, and be recognized in the New Years Honours List.

## Ingredients

* Wild Siberian Moose Milk
* Rennet from the fourth stomach of a Mongolian Yak
* Rock Salt from the deserted mines of Kazakhstan

**To register your place in the competition, please sign up with Mr Gordon Zola in the Royal Enclosure, where you will be fitted with a Great Moose Cheese Chase tracking device.**

*Note: Domesticated moose milk is unacceptable, along with rennet from any other stomach, or salt from another source.

The winner will be the first contestant to produce a moose cheese in time for the State Banquet. Should more than one contestant produce a cheese by the required date, Her Majesty the Queen will judge the winner by taste. The Queen's decision is final.

Employees of the Royal Household are ineligible to enter, as are their immediate families. Any such entries are invalid.

Under 18s must have parental or guardian consent.

The Queen began to speak again.

"I understand that you are all experienced in matters of cheese," she said. "However, Mr Gordon Zola will be on hand during the final process to help contestants make the moose cheese to my exact requirements. And finally, may I take this opportunity to wish you all the very best of luck."

The loud cheer from the crowd was drowned out by a roaring thump, thump, thump from the sky. The twins looked up to see a red, white and blue helicopter hovering above the fair. The tents and marquees started flapping furiously from the wind produced by the blades.

"What's that?" asked Bert, as a rope was slowly lowered down from the helicopter.

The twins watched as the Queen put her foot through a loop at the bottom of the rope. She clung on with one gloved hand and waved at the crowd with the other, her handbag wobbling in the downdraught.

"Isn't she marvellous," sighed Gramps, as the Queen soared up into the bright blue sky.

"Apparently, she's very into her extreme sports – snowboarding, skateboarding, keyboarding. . ."

"Wow!" cried Cam.

"Cool!" said Bert.

"God save the Queen!" shouted Gramps.

# 5

## The Forged Letter
### (Six days to go. . .)

The sound of the Queen's helicopter slowly faded and was replaced by the buzzing of the crowd. Whispers of *moose cheese* filled every tent and marquee. Cam noticed that several of the cheese stalls pulled down their shutters and had already begun to pack up. One of them was the man with the orange cheese that Gramps had been talking to earlier.

"Lester," called Gramps. "Are you leaving already? The fair has only just begun."

"No time to lose," said Lester. "This is a once-in-a-lifetime opportunity and I don't intend to miss it. I've signed up and have been given my Great Moose Cheese Chase tracking device." He held up a tiny moose-shaped transmitter and clipped it to his lapel. "I'm off to Siberia to find a wild moose. If I win, I will be Lord Lester."

"Do you mean to say, you're actually going to attempt to make a moose cheese?" asked Gramps.

"Of course!"

"But the ingredients are impossible to find!" cried Gramps. "You'll never be able to milk a wild moose! And don't tell me you're familiar with any Mongolian yaks. As for the salt – well, those mines in Kazakhstan are deserted for a reason!"

"Well, I'm going to try," Lester said, "and I'm not the only one. Take a look around you."

Gramps and the twins stood in the middle of the fair and watched as the excited crowd started to disperse. There was a large group of people surrounding Mr Zola in the royal enclosure, shouting for him to register them first. A white van zoomed past and screeched to a halt. Three men dressed from head to foot in white overalls and white sunglasses charged out of the royal enclosure and jumped in. The door slammed shut and the van took off.

"They're from the Specialist Cheesemakers Association," said Cam. "And they look like they know where they're going."

"I bet they've had a tip-off," said Lester, hooking his stall to the back of his car. "I've got to hurry. Wish me luck, Mr Curd. Bye, kids."

He sped off across the gorge with his cheese stall bobbing furiously behind him.

Bert tugged on Gramps' arm. "C'mon, Gramps! What are we waiting for?" he cried. "Let's sign up. I want to be Lord Curd."

"And I want to be Lady Camilla," said Cam. "You heard what Lester said – we're wasting time."

Gramps looked down at the two excited faces in front of him.

"We are not entering this competition," he said, "even if it is set by the Queen. It's far too dangerous.

Many people have died trying to make moose cheese. I promised your parents that I would—"

"—take care of us," interrupted Cam. "We know that. But if I was *Lady* Camilla then I could take care of you . . . and the farm. We would never have to worry about money again."

"I would rather lose the farm than you," he said. "It's completely out of the question – a fool's mission."

Just then, the two Easy Cheesy Doggy Treats men raced past on a tandem bike, their embroidered ears flying out behind them.

"Moose cheese, moose cheese, moose cheese!" they chanted.

Gramps folded his arms. "See!" he said. "I don't want to argue about it any more. We need to find the Show Tent. When my prize cheddar wins we won't need to worry about moose cheese."

The twins reluctantly followed Gramps inside the biggest marquee at the fair and immediately came face to face with Primula Mold. As well as the lucky Stilton around her neck, she was holding another blue cheese. She eyed them all suspiciously and clutched her cheese closer. Fungus waddled over to Bert, his long muddy ears flapping excitedly.

"Ah, Miss Mold," said Gramps. "Is that your prize cheese? Well, I hate to disappoint you, but this is mine."

He held up his cheddar, which was at least twice as big as Miss Mold's. She stared at the huge cheese.

"And I hate to disappoint *you*," she said, a thin wonky smile slowly stretching across her face. "But I'm withdrawing from the competition. I have better things to do."

Gramps' mouth dropped open. "Like what?"

"Like moose cheese," replied Miss Mold, holding up her tiny moose-transmitter.

Gramps' jaw fell another inch. "But we've been entering this competition for the last fifty years," he said.

"It's not about *this* competition any more," she croaked. "It's all about the other competition now. That's where the glory lies. I'm heading to Siberia right away and taking this cheese for supplies." She held up her prize blue cheese. "Are you coming?"

"No, I am not!"

Miss Mold's face dropped. "What do you mean?" she said. "You have to! We've been competing against each other for years and I want to beat you!"

"And I would love to beat you," replied Gramps. "But I can't leave the children."

"Take them with you, then," snapped Miss Mold. "I'm taking Fungus."

"That's not the same."

Miss Mold clenched her bony jaw and glared at the twins. "So be it," she said. "On my return you may address me as *Lady* Primula Mold. Maybe I'll buy up your land with the prize money and extend my blue cheese dairy. Of course, I would have to bulldoze that wreck of a farm of yours to make room for my goats, but it's almost falling down anyway. Goodbye, Mr Curd. Come, Fungus."

Fungus trotted after his mistress and out of the marquee.

"You mean old stick insect!" cried Bert.

"Now Bert, watch your manners," said Gramps.

"For once in my life I agree with Bert," grumbled Cam. "Why *is* she so mean?"

Gramps sighed and jingled his change.

"Time changes many things," he said. "Long ago, we used to be friends – sweethearts, even."

"Bleeuugggghhh!" cried Bert, clutching his throat and pretending to be sick. "That's gross!"

Gramps ignored him and carried on. "We grew up together and planned to join dairies and become a cheese force to be reckoned with. But then she became obsessed with the revolting art of blue cheese production. I could never agree to inject my cheese with mould, and we went our separate ways. Eventually, I met your grandmother and life went on. But Primula never forgave me and has been in fierce competition ever since."

"And now she wants to bulldoze our farm," cried Cam. "You can't let her get away with it, Gramps. We have to make that moose cheese first."

"Let's go, let's go!" said Bert, tugging Gramps' sleeve.

"Calm down. If I win 'Best Cheese in Show' then everything will be fine."

"Stop saying that everything will be fine!" wailed Cam. "Look around you! Everyone is going. Nobody cares about best in show any more. It's all about moose cheese now! If Primula Mold wins this competition then she can do whatever she likes. We will have to call her Lady Mold."

Gramps frowned and jingled loudly. "Part of me wants to go," he explained. "I would like nothing better than to beat that gloating old shrew. But like I mentioned before, it's far too dangerous, and I promised—"

"Don't you dare say it again," interrupted Cam.

"Besides," Gramps said, laughing, "how would we ever get to Siberia?"

"Miss Mold has obviously found a way," said Bert. "You two wait here while I go and see what she's up to."

"I'm coming too," said Cam, following him. "You're not going anywhere without me. I don't want you sneaking off to Siberia on your own."

Bert stopped and looked at her. "That's not a bad idea," he whispered.

They both glanced back at Gramps, who was fiddling with his prize cheddar.

"We'll be back in a minute," called Cam.

"Don't be long," said Gramps, holding his cheese up to the light.

They stepped outside just in time to see Primula Mold rise up into the blue sky in a bright yellow hot air balloon. Fungus' head popped up over the side of the basket, his ears swinging in the wind. They just caught sight of Miss Mold's smug face as she soared up and over the marquees, rubbing her lucky Stilton.

"She must have hired a balloon to take her to Siberia," said Cam. "I bet it cost a fortune."

They watched the large yellow globe shrink to the size of a lemon as it got further and further away.

"I've got to enter this competition," declared Bert, "with or without Gramps. Primula Mold must not win!"

"I can't let you go on your own," said Cam. "What if *you* win and get all the glory? I'm entering too."

"No! Your big butter-toes will just get in my way."

"It will be your pea-brain that gets in the way," snapped Cam. "You don't even know where Siberia is."

Bert frowned. "Somewhere near London?"

"Try northern Russia!"

"OK, smarty pants," he sniffed, "you can come as far as Russia with me if you can think of a way to get us there. Then we'll split up."

Cam rolled her eyes and took another look at the golden leaflet detailing the rules.

"Neither of us will be going anywhere unless we have Gramps' permission," she muttered. "We need a letter from him to get registered, and that's not going to happen."

They stood for a moment staring at the rules.

"I've got an idea," murmured Bert, looking all around him.

"That's a first," said Cam.

"You could do it," he whispered. "You could write the letter of consent and sign it from Gramps. I would do it but my writing looks like a load of squashed flies."

"I'm not forging a letter!" cried Cam. "That's cheating! Gramps would be furious."

"He would soon forgive us when we arrive home with all the ingredients for the moose cheese," said Bert. "I think Gramps wants us to enter the competition – he just doesn't know it yet. He said that part of him would like to go. Well, *we* are part of him – *we* are his grandchildren. The only reason he won't give us a real letter of consent is because he thinks collecting the ingredients will be too dangerous. But if we ask him *after* we get them all, then everything will be OK. This letter is just temporary. We need it to get registered."

"I don't know," sighed Cam. "He's still going to be mad if we leave without telling him."

Bert shook his head. "The most important thing is that Gramps would like nothing better than to beat Primula Mold," he said. "So, one of us has to win this competition – for him!"

Cam nodded slowly. "OK," she said, looking over her shoulder to make sure no one was watching. "You're right."

She pulled a pen out of her pocket, turned the leaflet over and wrote carefully on the back.

*To Whom It May Concern:*

*I, Cornelius Curd, give my consent as legal guardian for Camilla and Bert Curd to take part in The Great Moose Cheese Chase.*

*Yours sincerely,*

*C. Curd*

"I'm impressed," whispered Bert. "You're normally such a goody-goody."

Cam turned pink.

"I'm doing this for Gramps!" she hissed. "Come on, let's see if it works."

They walked towards the royal enclosure, past three huge hot air balloons tethered to the ground. One of them was the Crown Balloon. Its large golden basket was tied to four posts with red satin ropes. They stopped to look inside. A golden throne with a cushioned seat took up the whole of one end. The basket was completely lined with purple velvet. Cam ran her hand over the plush material.

"Even if we register, how are we going to get to Siberia?" she said. "We can't afford one of these."

They peered in. A gilded framework held up the burners, which sat between the enormous basket and the canopy. Two golden lions stood to attention either side of the throne. Beside one of them was an ivory side table with a small bowl of peppermints and a couple of magazines on top – *Horse and Hound* and *Extreme Bungee Jumping*. At the other end was a large wooden chest, a solar-powered kettle and a silver tea service.

"It's massive," said Bert. "Big enough to have a party in. . . Big enough to . . . hide in."

They turned at the sound of approaching voices. Mr Zola, the Royal Cheesemaker, came striding towards them, followed by two attendants. He was studying a large round radar device attached to his wrist.

"My Cheesemaker-Locator has indicated that some of the contestants have already left for Russia," he said to the attendants. "I have to follow and report back to the Queen. The wind is perfect and I must leave immediately."

Bert stepped forward.

"Excuse me," he said, "but my sister and I would like to register for the competition."

"I'm afraid you're too late, young man," said Mr Zola, climbing into the basket. "Registration is now closed. Release the ropes!"

The two men started to untie the Crown Balloon from its mooring.

"Stop!" cried Bert in alarm. "It can't be closed. We have to enter. You don't understand!"

Mr Zola twiddled his moustache irritably. "If I say it's closed, then it's closed," he said, as the great balloon began to rise from the ground. "The Queen herself has put me in charge of this competition. She placed this cheese hat on my head with her very own bejewelled fingers and said—"

"What hat?" asked Bert.

Mr Zola's hands flew up to his bare head. "My cheese hat!" he yelled. "Pull me back in. I must have left it in the royal enclosure."

Cam and Bert watched as the men caught hold of the ropes and heaved the huge balloon back into place. Mr Zola jumped out.

"Help me find it," he called to the attendants. "I can't be late."

The twins looked at each other as the three men disappeared round the corner.

"What shall we do?" whispered Cam.

"Quick, into the basket," answered Bert. "This is our only chance. We'll have to stow away and try and persuade Mr Zola to register us for the competition on the way."

They clambered in and looked around. Cam lifted up the lid of the big wooden chest. Inside was a fur rug, some warm coats and a union jack parachute. She pulled out the rug and threw it to Bert.

"Put that over you and hide under the throne," she said, stepping into the chest. "I can just about fit in here."

She closed the lid as Bert squeezed beneath the large seat. They both crouched in their hiding places, their hearts beating wildly. Bert began to fidget.

"Cam?" he called.

"Yes?"

"I'm having second thoughts."

"What!"

"I'm not sure this is such a good idea," he said. "Is it sunny in Siberia?"

But before she could answer, Mr Zola had returned with his cheese hat and climbed back into the basket. The two attendants released the red satin ropes and the Crown Balloon floated high up into the sky.

# 6

## Gordon Zola

Bert lay flat under the throne, the fur rug covering his body. His palms were sweating and he felt sick. Had they just made a terrible mistake? Mr Zola was sitting above him on the large cushioned seat.

Cam lifted the chest lid a centimetre and peeped out. She was beginning to regret what they'd done too. What would Mr Zola do when he found out he had a couple of stowaways? And Gramps was going to be hopping mad.

She watched Mr Zola let down two ear flaps attached to his cheese hat. It was getting colder as they climbed higher. He produced a hand mirror from a fringed leather bag and studied himself, stroking his moustache and murmuring something under his breath. Then he checked his Cheesemaker-Locator and began springing gently up and down on the throne. Cam could see Bert's head being gently pummelled by Mr Zola's bottom. Bert let out an involuntary squeak. Mr Zola leapt to his feet and glared at the throne suspiciously.

"Did you hear that, Monty?" he said.

Cam glanced around the basket to see who "Monty" was, but there appeared to be no one else there. Mr Zola got to his knees and peered under the throne. He produced a long telescope and began poking the fur rug with it.

"Gerr-off," mumbled Bert.

Mr Zola let out a small scream and ran to the other side of the basket.

"Who's there?" he shrieked, holding the telescope up like a sword. "Show yourself!"

Bert crawled out from under the throne, his green eyes wide with panic and his mouth pulled in that strange diagonal line.

"A stowaway!" gasped Mr Zola.

"Erm . . . t-two, actually," stuttered Cam, popping up from her hiding place.

Mr Zola spun round as Cam tried to climb out of the crate, tripped on the side and fell in a heap on the floor.

"I think I'm going to faint," mumbled Mr Zola, raising the back of his hand to his forehead. "Quick, fetch my man-bag."

As he slid theatrically to the floor, he managed to point to the fringed leather bag.

Bert and Cam looked at each other in confusion before grabbing the bag. They knelt beside the crumpled Mr Zola.

"Smelling salts," he moaned.

Bert peered into the bag and pulled out a small bottle. He held it under Mr Zola's nose.

"Mind the moustache," said Mr Zola, snatching the bottle and inhaling deeply.

The twins wrinkled their noses as the smell of lavender oil and ammonia drifted out. Mr Zola pushed himself up into a sitting position and pulled out the small mirror from his man-bag. He checked his reflection before turning to the twins.

"You are in so much trouble!" he hissed. "Do you realize what you've done?"

"We're so sorry," murmured Bert. "We were hoping to—"

"I don't care what you were hoping to do!" shouted Mr Zola. He turned back to the mirror and patted the curly hair on his top lip. "You've tangled the 'tache!"

"Pardon?" asked Cam.

"You've mangled my muzzie!" he fumed. "Niggled my nose neighbour!"

Cam frowned.

"You and your silly escapades have messed up my moustache!" ranted Mr Zola, twiddling his elaborate nose hair back into place. "Poor Monty! He gets very nervous around children."

"Monty?" repeated Cam. "Your moustache has a name?"

"Of course he has a name," he cried, getting to his feet. "But what's *your* name? Who are you? You are trespassing on Her Majesty's property!"

Cam cleared her throat and glanced nervously at Bert.

"M-my name is Camilla Curd and this is my brother, Bert," she said hesitantly. "First of all, we would like to apologize for scaring your moustache."

Bert looked at her as if she was mad, but Mr Zola seemed pleased with the apology.

"I've n-never seen such a fine moustache," she went on. "Have you, Bert?"

A small smile touched Mr Zola's face as he coaxed "Monty" round into two perfectly symmetrical coils.

"Erm . . . no," said Bert. "It's really . . . I mean, *he* is really . . . um . . . hairy. Is he friendly?"

The smile beneath Mr Zola's moustache vanished. "Not with trespassers," he warned.

"We're very sorry for hiding in the Crown Balloon," said Cam. "But when you said that registration was closed, we panicked. You see, we have to win this competition. If we don't we could lose our home."

"Everyone has their reasons for wanting to win this competition," snapped Mr Zola. "And your problems are none of my concern. How dare you hide in the Crown Balloon? I can't be held back by a couple of stowaways. I'm on a mission for the Queen. And now I have to return to the World Cheese Fair and have you arrested. It's a complete waste of my time. And Her Majesty's, I might add."

"Arrested?" cried Bert. "No! Wait! We're really sorry."

Mr Zola ignored him and took out the long telescope.

"How infuriating," he tutted, looking all around. "We can't turn back because the wind is in the wrong direction and we can't go down as we're right over the English Channel."

"If you can't take us back, then take us with you," pleaded Bert. "If you register us now and then drop us off in Siberia, you won't have wasted any time at all."

"We promise not to get in your way," added Cam. "You won't even know we're here."

"Impossible!" said Mr Zola. "Under eighteens must have the consent of a parent or guardian."

"We have a letter from our grandpa," said Cam, crossing her fingers behind her back.

"Not good enough," replied Mr Zola. "Like I said, it has to be from parents or guardians."

"Gramps is our guardian," said Bert. "We don't have any parents. They died years ago in a terrible cheese accident."

Cam noticed Mr Zola's face soften. He put down the telescope and eyed them warily.

"I too lost a parent in a cheese-related accident," he muttered, lifting a manicured hand to his lip.

He began to stroke a quivering Monty. Cam's eyes swivelled towards Bert before returning to Mr Zola.

"Ours were fatally injured in an annual cheese-rolling competition," she said, gently. "They were chasing a round cheese down a very steep hill. It can reach speeds of up to seventy miles per hour. Our parents were very competitive and determined to catch the cheese first. Unfortunately they collided. The coroner's verdict was 'death by cheese'."

They all stared at the floor of the balloon.

"But our Gramps looks after us now," said Bert. "He's the best cheese farmer in the country and he sent us on this competition . . . sort of."

"What happened to your mum or dad?" asked Cam.

Mr Zola pulled a lace hanky from his man-bag and dabbed his eyes. "My poor papa was also the Royal Cheesemaker – one of those who died on a moose cheese quest."

The twins gasped.

"Our most royal and noble Queen has desired a moose cheese for a long time," he sniffed. "It is the rarest of the rare; a delicacy beyond most people's grasp. My father died trying to milk a wild moose. It turned out to be a bull and he was killed by a single kick to the head. I never knew my mother, so I was brought up in the royal household."

He blew his nose on the lacy hanky and stuffed it back in his man-bag. "I'm afraid it's left me with a fear of mooses. I mean, a fear of meese. I mean, a . . . what do I mean?"

Cam put her arm around him and gave him a pat on the back. "I know exactly what you mean – moose," she said. "How are you going to cope in Siberia? What if you bump into one?"

"I plan to watch from afar," he said, holding up the telescope. "I can still let Her Majesty know what's going on without going near one of the beasts."

"We could help you if you like," said Bert. "We're always happy to help out a fellow cheese-orphan, aren't we, Cam?"

She nodded enthusiastically.

"I work alone," said Mr Zola. "Apart from Monty, of course."

"Monty's looking a lot calmer now," said Cam. "I think he's getting used to us. . . *Please* can we register, Mr Zola? Here's the letter of consent from our grandpa."

She handed him the golden leaflet. Mr Zola frowned and read the fake note written on the back. He hesitated for a moment before pulling out a rolled-up scroll from his man-bag.

"This is highly irregular," he said, "but your story has moved me. I suppose I could make an exception for those who have also suffered at the hands of cheese. Besides, I can't afford to waste any more time."

Mr Zola scanned the note again.

"So, just to double check – as legal guardian, your grandfather gives his permission for you to take part in the Great Moose Cheese Chase – correct?"

"He does," murmured Cam, glancing anxiously at Bert.

"He will," he whispered.

Mr Zola ticked a box. "Sign here, please."

He unrolled the scroll of paper. It had a long list of names. The twins looked at each other with a mix of terror and excitement before signing their names at the bottom.

"I'm logging you in the Cheesemaker-Locator under CT for 'Curd Twins'," he said, tapping the screen of the tracking device attached to his wrist.

"Here is your transmitter."

He handed Cam a tiny moose-shaped locator. "These allow me to keep tabs on everyone's progress. I plan to keep abreast with the leaders and report back to the Queen."

"Where's mine?" asked Bert. "We want to enter as separate competitors. How do you even know we're twins?"

Mr Zola raised his eyebrows. "It's quite obvious," he sighed. "You look just like each other."

Cam and Bert both gasped in horror.

"There's no need to be rude," spluttered Bert.

Mr Zola shook his head and continued tapping the Cheesemaker-locator. "I can enter you separately if you wish," he said. "BC for Bert and CC for Camilla."

Bert nodded and accepted his transmitter.

"Why aren't *you* making a moose cheese?" he asked, clipping it to his pocket. "After all, you're the Royal Cheesemaker."

"Nobody from the royal household is allowed to take part," he explained. "It would be unfair.

Besides, I have the most important job of all. The Queen has entrusted me to return home with the first person who gets all the ingredients. Then I will make sure that the moose cheese is made to Her Highness's exact requirements. Ultimately, I am the only cheesemaker she trusts."

"You don't get much of the glory, though, do you?" said Bert. "Don't you want to be a lord? And what about the prize money?"

"Some things are worth more than money, young man. The look on my beloved sovereign's face when she bites into that moose cheese will be reward enough for me."

Cam took a deep breath as the balloon dipped in the wind. She looked over the basket for the first time. There were clouds below and she couldn't see the ground. She felt the butterflies rise in her stomach and shivered.

"I've got a feeling I'm going to win," she sighed. "I'm good at making cheese. Last year I was runner-up in the Junior Cheddar Championships."

"Yes, *runner-up!*" cried Bert. "You didn't win then

and you're not going to win now. I am."

"I am!"

"I am!"

"I—"

"Stop that!" interrupted Mr Zola. "Monty's bristles are extremely noise-sensitive. He gets very agitated, and believe me, you don't want to see him when he's angry."

He got to his feet and opened the big wooden chest.

"Here," he said, throwing them two fur-lined jackets. "You'll need coats where we're going."

They were too big, but lovely and warm. Mr Zola pulled a long black coat around his own shoulders.

"Now, I have to report back to the Queen, so keep quiet. I don't want her knowing that I've acquired a couple of stowaways."

He produced a red mobile phone from his man-bag and pushed a button.

"Your Majesty," he simpered. "May I say how glorious and radiant you are sounding this evening? I trust you had a good helicopter flight back to the palace?" There was a pause as he listened to the reply. ". . .And your parachute opened OK? . . . Did your corgi enjoy the tandem jump? . . . Jolly good show, ma'am. . . Well, there's not much to report as yet. Several groups of cheesemakers have set off already and I should make Russia by tomorrow morning."

The twins pulled their coats around them and looked up at the sky.

"I've got butterflies in my tummy," whispered Cam.

Bert nodded. "I've got golden eagles in mine," he muttered.

It was hard to believe, but they were going to Siberia. They were officially part of the Great Moose Cheese Chase.

# 7

## St Basil's Cathedral

After spending the night floating across the north European sky under the fur rug, the twins were jolted awake by a loud crash. Their blanket was thrown off and they toppled over each other, landing on top of a sleepy Mr Zola.

"Watch the whiskers," he grunted, pushing the twins off.

The basket was tilting at a worrying angle. They all looked up into the dawn sky to see the flame above the gas canister had gone out and the huge Crown Balloon was slowly deflating.

"The fire's out!" screamed Mr Zola. "We're going to crash!"

"But we're not moving," said Bert, getting to his feet. "And look, we're surrounded by other hot air balloons."

Right beside the basket were the tops of several large domes. They looked like giant onions, each with a bulbous middle tapering smoothly to a point. They were beautifully ornate. Some were dotted with gold, green and crimson, and others were striped yellow and green, or blue and white.

"Why aren't we plummeting to our deaths?" asked Mr Zola, clutching his smelling salts in one hand and Monty in the other.

Cam peeped over the edge of the basket. "These aren't balloons," she gasped. "They're the tops of towers. We've crashed into an enormous building."

Bert and Mr Zola joined Cam and looked down at the city below.

"I do believe that we have landed in Red Square, Moscow," announced Mr Zola, inhaling deeply from his smelling salts. "And we are dangling precariously from St Basil's Cathedral. We must have blown off course last night."

"Where's Moscow?" asked Bert.

"It's the capital of Russia," said Cam.

"Know-it-all," muttered Bert.

"And St Basil's Cathedral is the jewel in Moscow's crown," continued Cam. "It was built on the city's geometric centre, four hundred and fifty years ago, by Ivan the Terrible."

"Well, he wasn't terrible at building cathedrals," said Bert. "It's amazing."

"B-beautiful it may be," stuttered Mr Zola. "But how are we going to get down? We must be at least fifty metres off the ground."

Bert felt his stomach tighten as he looked over the edge. He wasn't scared of heights and he knew Cam wasn't either. But if anything happened to them, then Gramps would be left on his own and the farm could be lost. He wasn't going to let that happen.

"How many ties has this balloon got?" he asked, picking up one of the red satin ropes that secured the balloon to the ground.

"Four," replied Mr Zola. "But please don't tell me you're thinking of climbing down St Basil's on a rope."

"No, not climb."

"Thank goodness for that."

"Abseil!"

Mr Zola's eyes widened and his hands flew up to his moustache.

"Monty doesn't like heights," he said in a small voice.

Cam looked down at the ground below, a small gasp escaping from her diagonal mouth.

"OK," she said slowly. "We've got to get down somehow. I'll need some of that rope to make harnesses."

Bert began to cut the other three ropes and tie them securely together.

"It's all right, Mr Zola," he said. "Once we've got the ropes all fitted, there should only be about a seven-metre drop to the ground – about the same as the first storey of a house."

There was a thump as Mr Zola's legs buckled.

"He needs those smelling salts tied around

his neck," whispered Cam.

Eventually the long single rope was lowered over the basket and the three of them stood with their makeshift harnesses around their waists.

"Don't be scared, Mr Zola," said Cam, patting him encouragingly on the back. "Bert and I do lots of climbing and abseiling where we live in Cheddar Gorge."

"I'm f-fine," stammered Mr Zola. "It's M-Monty I'm worried about."

The twins exchanged a look before Bert climbed out of the basket.

"We're going to have to use an old-fashioned method of abseiling," he said. "You have to wrap your harness around the top of your legs and waist to make a seat and firmly tie it to the main rope. The friction between the two ropes should stop you falling. Then, lean back and gently ease yourself down, using your legs to bounce off the walls. I'll go first as I'm the best abseiler."

"You are not!" snapped Cam. "I'm best, I

should go first."

She tried to climb over Bert but he wouldn't let her pass.

"I'm going first! This was my idea," yelled Bert.

There was an awkward scuffle and the basket lurched dangerously to one side, knocking Mr Zola off his feet.

"Stop fighting!" he screamed. "Camilla, you must go last. I need to be in the middle of you both. Now, let's get going before Monty changes his mind!"

They set off down the rope, Bert first, followed by Mr Zola and Cam last. The wind whistled through their hair. Nobody dared to look down. The rope swayed from side to side, knocking them against the cathedral wall. It was hard work and their hands were sore. About halfway along, the basket above them jolted and slipped down. Cam lost her grip and slid down the rope, bumping against the top of Mr Zola's head.

"You clumsy oaf," he squawked. "The situation is bad enough without you squashing my cheese hat."

Just then, the red phone in Mr Zola's man-bag

started to play "God Save the Queen".

"I don't believe it," he spluttered. "It's her!"

He carefully pulled out the phone with one hand while gripping tightly to the rope with the other.

"Your Majesty. . . Yes, everything is fine," he said, looking down at the lethal drop below him. "I'm just . . . hanging around in Moscow. . . The Crown Balloon, ma'am? . . . Erm, I need to talk to you about that. . . Yes, of course. . . I will be there as soon as possible . . . no more delays . . . goodbye, ma'am."

He replaced the phone. "I've got to get to Siberia immediately," he said. "But I couldn't bring myself to tell her about the Crown Balloon just yet. She's going to be furious."

"There's nothing you can do about it now," said Cam. "Let's just get to the ground. I can feel the basket wobbling above us. It doesn't feel very safe."

Mr Zola closed his eyes and clung tightly to his rope. "You're scaring Monty," he whimpered.

"There's nothing to worry about," called Bert from below. "Only twenty-five per cent of all climbing deaths happen while abseiling."

"THAT'S NOT HELPING!" screamed Mr Zola.

After spending several minutes urging Mr Zola to loosen his grip, they slowly continued their descent of St Basil's Cathedral. The twins marvelled at the intricate patterns made by the red brickwork and the shiny globes that topped the numerous domes like golden cherries. They caught glimpses of bright mosaics through the narrow windows and called to Mr Zola to open his eyes and look. But he kept them tightly shut the whole way.

"We're nearly at the bottom," shouted Bert, after several minutes. "And it looks like we've got a welcoming committee."

Cam looked down to see that a small crowd had gathered below. She could hear them chattering in Russian. Suddenly, one of the crowd screamed and pointed up at the cathedral. Cam heard a rumble and felt the rope go slack. She looked up to see the golden basket slip from its mooring. But before she could gather her thoughts, she dropped like a sack of potatoes.

# 8

## Moose Fleas

Cam opened her eyes. It was pitch black. A dull ache drifted up her legs, but luckily it felt like she had landed on something soft. She reached beneath her to see what it was. Her hand touched something warm and hairy.

"Lay off the lip warmer," said a voice.

"Mr Zola! Are you all right?"

The basket that covered them began to tip up and light came streaming in. Cam found herself sitting on top of Mr Zola, who was laid out flat on his back. Bert, helped by several people, was pushing the basket over.

"Cam!" he shouted. "You're OK!"

"Yes," she said, "but I'm not sure about Mr Zola. What happened?"

"We were closer to the ground than I thought," said Bert. "I managed to dive out of the way when the basket fell on top of you two. Thank goodness it landed upside down."

Mr Zola groaned and sat up. "I'm OK," he moaned. "But I think Monty might have broken a bristle. Someone call an ambulance."

"Monty looks fine," said Cam. "But listen. I can hear sirens. Someone must have called an ambulance already."

The wailing of the siren got louder and the excited crowd opened up to let the vehicle through. But it wasn't an ambulance. It was a car with the white, blue and red flag of Russia emblazoned on the bonnet and the word POLITSIYA underneath. A blue and orange light flashed on the roof.

"It's the police," said Mr Zola, staggering to his feet. "Let me handle this; my Russian is pretty good."

Two officers got out of the car dressed in light blue shirts and large caps with red bands round the middle. A woman from the crowd stepped forward. She was talking quickly in Russian, pointing up at St Basil's Cathedral and then at the twins and the basket. Mr Zola stepped between them and cleared his throat. He was still wearing his cheese hat, although it was crumpled and covered in dust. He started speaking Russian. There were lots of pauses and "um"s and "er"s but the twins thought he was doing very well. The police officers were frowning as they listened and occasionally glanced over at the twins and then at each other. One of them held his hand up for Mr Zola to stop talking and approached the children.

"Are you OK?" he asked, in a thick Russian accent.

"Yes," said the twins together.

"My name is Officer Sergei and I speak a little English."

He gestured to Mr Zola. "Your father is mad, no?"

"He isn't our father," said Cam.

"But he *is* mad," added Bert.

"He tell us he make fleas for the Queen of England and she has sent him on a mission to find a moose flea. Is this correct?"

"No," cried Bert. "It's cheese – moose cheese."

"Ah," said Officer Sergei, looking Mr Zola up and down. "He also claims to have pet moustache."

"I'm afraid that's correct," sighed Cam.

"I did not say 'pet'," gasped Mr Zola. "He is my friend and loyal companion."

Officer Sergei shook his head and pulled out some handcuffs.

"OK, I have heard enough about moose fleas and friendly moustaches," he said. "I take you to police station for questioning. You enter my country illegally and may have damaged our precious cathedral. The children will come too."

"What?" screeched Mr Zola. "But I'm telling the truth! We are part of the Great Moose Cheese Chase. The Queen has cleared our arrival in Siberia with your president."

"This is not Siberia," stated Officer Sergei, fastening a handcuff to Mr Zola's wrist.

The twins watched in alarm.

"We weren't meant to land here," said Bert. "We blew off course."

"And it's true about the Queen," added Cam. "So if we've accidentally caused any damage then she'll pay for everything."

Officer Sergei attached the other handcuff to his own wrist.

"My colleague is checking your story with the authorities," he said, looking over at the other policeman, who was deep in conversation on his radio. "For now, you come to police station."

He began pulling Mr Zola towards the police car.

"But I have to get to Siberia," wailed Mr Zola.

Officer Sergei opened the car door just as his colleague replaced the receiver. The two policemen began talking rapidly in Russian. After a minute Officer Sergei unlocked the handcuffs.

"It seems you tell truth," he said. "My colleague has confirmed your story with Buckingham Palace, Interpol and Intercheese. But you must still get in car. Your queen is not happy about balloon."

He pointed up at the deflated canopy that waved from one of St Basil's towers like a huge flag.

"We have instructions to take you to station."

"Are you going to arrest us?" asked Bert.

"Arrest? No! I take you to *train* station. You are heading north on world-famous Trans-Siberian Railway."

Cam clapped her hands. She had read about the Trans-Siberian Railway – the longest track in the world, with links running as far as China to the east and Mongolia to the south. It passed through some of the most beautiful and rugged terrain on earth.

"Wait a minute," cried Mr Zola. "It's me that the Queen needs to get to Siberia, not these two." He stood in front of the car door, blocking their way. "They're just stowaways."

Officer Sergei frowned deeply. "What am I supposed to do with them?" he asked.

"I don't know," said Mr Zola. "They're not my responsibility."

Officer Sergei took his hat off and glared at Mr Zola.

"Sir," he said, sternly, "you arrive in my country with two children and a pet moustache. Are you going to tell me that the moustache is no longer your responsibility too?"

"Of course not," answered Mr Zola, grabbing Monty defensively.

"Then you leave with the moustache *and* the two children. They are all your responsibility now."

Mr Zola grudgingly moved aside so the twins could climb into the back of the police car and squeezed in beside them.

"If I must," he sighed.

The car set off, sirens blasting and lights flashing.

"Woohoo!" shouted Bert. "I've always wanted a ride in a speeding police car."

"Ow!" cried Cam. "Mr Zola, you're hurting my arm."

Mr Zola was clinging to Cam's arm as they sped through the streets of Moscow.

"Don't tell me," she said, "Monty doesn't like going fast."

"You're getting to know him very well," whispered Mr Zola. "Do we really need to go at this pace?"

"Yes, we do," called Officer Sergei from the driver's seat. "Your queen has made clear you cannot be missing nine fifteen train from Moscow Central. It leaves in two minutes. The next one isn't till day after tomorrow. If we fail, she cut off my head."

He turned and winked at Cam.

"How long till we get there?" shrieked Mr Zola as they skidded round a corner, knocking a bin flying and scattering the pedestrians.

"About three minutes," said Officer Sergei.

"But I thought you said the train left in two."

"Yes, but I have plan."

"Are you going to call ahead and delay departure?" asked Mr Zola, resuming his hold on Cam's bruised arm.

"No, no!" shouted Officer Sergei. "No one, not even your queen, can delay Trans-Siberian train. We catch it up and drive beside at exactly the same speed. Then I open hatch in roof of car and you climb out and jump aboard. Easy!"

"Are you mad?" cried Mr Zola. "We can't do that!"

"Then you must wait for next train."

Bert tried to swallow, but his mouth was completely dry.

"We can't wait that long," he croaked. "We have no choice."

Cam nodded slowly as Mr Zola crumpled in a heap on her lap.

After a couple of minutes the road turned a bend and ran directly beside the railway track.

"There she is," called Officer Sergei.

The twins looked out of the window to see a train speeding along the track ahead of them. The carriages were white on top, blue in the middle and red on the bottom, just like the Russian flag.

"We're catching it up," cried Bert. "Have you revived Mr Zola yet?"

"He's getting there," said Cam, popping the top back on to the smelling salts. "Mr Zola, if you miss this train then the Queen's going to be in a right royal rage. We've got to do it."

Mr Zola sat up and looked at the speeding train. His face was white.

"OK, we're up to speed," shouted Officer Sergei. "Out you go! Good luck!"

Cam was suddenly glad of Mr Zola's clinging fingers. The discomfort in her arm was taking her mind off what was to come. Now was definitely not the time to be clumsy. But she had to get to Siberia, and she had to get there fast.

"I'm going first," she said, breaking away from Mr Zola and poking her head through the sunroof.

"No, I am," cried Bert, pulling her back in. "You'll just fall off."

"I will not!"

"You're too clumsy."

"I am not! It's my turn to go first!"

"For goodness' sake!" shouted Mr Zola. "I would rather die than listen to you two bicker again! No wonder your poor grandfather sent you to Siberia! I will go first!"

He pushed past Cam and pulled himself through the hatch and on to the roof of the car. "This is for my dear Papa!" he called.

"And for our dear Gramps," gulped Cam, scrambling up after him. Bert followed close behind. The wind screeched past their faces, whipping up their hair. The sound of the roaring train beside them was deafening. Mr Zola was holding on to the flashing light on top of the car. He had secured his cheese hat firmly to his head with the two ear flaps, but Monty was flapping dangerously around his terrified face. He held out his hand to Cam, who in turn grabbed Bert. They managed to get to their feet.

"OK!" yelled Mr Zola. "JUUUUUUMP!"

# The Trans-Siberian Railway

Mr Zola screamed as he let go of Cam's hand and flung himself at the speeding train. He managed to catch hold of a rail that ran along the roof. Cam jumped next, grabbing the same rail and hauling herself up on to the top of the train. She looked across for Bert. He wasn't there.

"BERT!" she shouted in panic. But her cries were lost in the roar of the train and the blast of the wind.

She lay down flat on her stomach and peered over the edge, still holding tightly to the rail. To her relief, there was Bert, clinging precariously to the top of a window, his legs swinging to the side with the force of the wind. Cam tried to stretch down with her arm but couldn't reach.

"Help me," she cried to Mr Zola. "I can't reach Bert. My arms aren't long enough."

Mr Zola was clutching the rail with both hands and legs, the tassels on his man-bag thrashing madly in the wind.

"I would if I had another arm," he screeched, "but I'm afraid I only have two."

Cam looked back down at Bert. To her horror, she realized that he'd lost his grip and was now just clinging on with one hand.

"Hold on, Bert! I'm coming!"

She turned around and lowered her legs down, still gripping tightly to the rail. She jammed her feet just above the window frame.

"Grab my legs," she shouted. "I've got a good hold."

The wind carried her voice away, but Bert could see what she was trying to do and managed to grab her ankle with his spare hand.

"Climb up me," she yelled. "Try and get in through the window."

Somehow, he pulled himself level with the window and knocked against the glass. He waited for a moment and banged again before continuing to climb up Cam.

"I'm all right," he shouted. "But I can't get the attention of the people inside. We'll have to get back on the roof."

He used Cam's head as a foothold and pushed himself up. Then he reached down and heaved Cam up beside him. They lay flat on top of the train, gasping for breath.

"The three men from the Specialist Cheesemakers Association are inside the carriage," panted Bert. "They didn't see or hear me because they all had their heads deep in books – *How to Catch a Moose*, *Moose Training Tips* and *The Three Mooseketeers*."

"We've got to beat them," puffed Cam. "But how are we going to get inside the train now?"

"We'll have to try another window . . . and Cam . . .

maybe you haven't got butter-toes after all . . . thanks."

Cam smiled, despite the fact that they were whizzing through the Russian countryside, clinging to the top of a train. She was just getting her breath back when Bert gave a shout and pointed to the sky. She looked up to see a bright yellow balloon sail above them, heading in the opposite direction.

"Primula Mold!" she cried.

Bert nodded. "But she's going the wrong way," he yelled.

They were interrupted by a shout from Mr Zola. "Over here," he called.

He had dragged himself along the rail and was pointing to a hatch in the roof. The twins followed. Bert reached across, undid the bolt and pulled it open. Cam managed to prise Mr Zola off his rail and shove him through the hole. She quickly followed, with Bert right behind. They landed in a large mound of hay.

"The standard in these Trans-Siberian carriages is not at all what I was expecting," sniffed Mr Zola, raising his lace hanky to his nose.

The carriage was dim. The only light came from

two small windows set high in the wall. There were no interconnecting doors to the rest of the train, only a huge sliding gate which took up the whole of one side. Thick stalks of straw were scattered on the floor, hiding great lumps of steaming dung. Mr Zola resumed his grasp on Cam's arm as a large shadow moved across the front of the carriage and a terrible wailing moo-growl burst out of the gloom.

"Mmmmooooooooaaaahhhhrrrrrr!"

Mr Zola screamed as a gigantic bulbous muzzle loomed up above them.

"MOOSE!" he shrieked, frantically trying to jump back up on to the roof.

Shocked by its unexpected visitors, and unnerved by the thin man jumping up and down in front of it, the moose began to moo-growl louder, stamping its feet and swinging its huge head from side to side.

"Mmmmooooooooaaaahhhhrrrrrr!"

"It's going to charge," yelled Mr Zola, hopping manically round the carriage. "We were safer on the roof."

"Stop it!" shouted Bert. "You're scaring it."

"*I'm* scaring *it*?" screamed Mr Zola.

"Yes, now get a grip!"

Mr Zola shrank into a corner and covered himself in hay. The moose calmed down and backed off to the rear of the carriage, eyeing the twins warily. It really was the strangest creature they had ever seen. Its four long spindly legs didn't look strong enough to support the huge body and even bigger head. Two great antlers stuck out from either side, framing a nose the size of a dinner plate.

"What's it doing on a train?" asked Bert, looking around the carriage.

There were several bales of hay and a bucket of water with a couple of empty bottles beside it. The bucket had a panda stamped on the side.

"Look," said Cam. "That's the sign for the World Wildlife Foundation. They must be relocating the moose. Maybe they're taking it back to the wild.

Bert slowly walked towards the moose and held out his hand. "It's OK, big fella," he said, gently. "We're not going to hurt you."

The moose snorted suspiciously before sniffing his hand. Very gently, Bert began stroking its huge muzzle.

"I see why you're so nervous," he whispered. "You're not a 'fella' at all, are you? Cam, come here and look."

From out of the gloom a tiny moose calf ventured from beneath its mother, its dark, worried eyes flicking from one child to the other.

"And where there's a moose calf. . ." said Bert.

"There's moose milk," finished Cam.

# 10

## Moose Milk

"Did someone mention moose milk?" asked Mr Zola, popping his head out of the hay.

"Yes," said Bert, still gently stroking the enormous moose, "and we have to make friends with this lovely lady if we're going to get any."

"Impossible! I've already explained that I'm moose-phobic. Poor Monty will turn white if we have to stay in this carriage a moment longer."

"He already has," giggled Cam.

Mr Zola whipped out a hand mirror from his man-bag and studied his moustache. It was covered in hay.

"Monty!" he chided. "You're a disgrace!"

He produced a silver pair of tweezers and began picking out every strand of hay. Cam turned to Bert.

"I can't believe he's telling his moustache off," she whispered.

"Just let him get on with it," said Bert. "Let's concentrate on getting some moose milk. It must be just like milking a cow at home . . . but bigger . . . much bigger. I'll keep her distracted while you milk her."

Cam looked around for something to put the milk in and spotted the empty water bottles lying beside the bucket. She grabbed them both and walked slowly towards the mother moose. But when it saw her coming the moose pulled away from Bert and trotted towards its baby with a great, "Mmmmooooooooaaaahhhhhrrrrrr!"

Cam staggered back and Mr Zola disappeared under the hay again. Bert sighed and held his hand out to the baby.

"C'mon, little one," he whispered. "If you come closer then maybe your mum will too. We just want to share some of your milk."

The calf tottered over on its skinny little legs and nuzzled against Bert. It was closely followed by its mother.

"There we go," he said, tickling two pairs of silky ears. "Quickly, Cam. Do it now, while I've got both of them."

Cam tried again but every time she came close, the mother moose shied away. "She won't let me near her."

"Try harder," cried Bert. "I can't do everything myself."

"You can't do *anything* by yourself!" spluttered Cam. "You wouldn't have even got this far if it wasn't for me."

"Would."

"Wouldn't."

"Would."

"You didn't even know where Siberia was!"

"Did."

"Didn't."

"Did."

Suddenly, Mr Zola sprang from the hay.

"Stop it!" he wailed. "Your incessant bickering is driving me crazy!"

The mother moose swung her enormous head round and looked straight at Mr Zola. She grunted softly and took a step towards him.

"She's staring at Monty," he gulped, edging back.

The moose made a low snuffling sound and slowly nudged against him.

"What does she want?"

"I think she likes you," said Bert.

Mr Zola was now backed against the wall with the huge moose sniffing his cheese hat.

"She's going to eat me," he said in a terrified whisper.

"Quick," said Bert, "let's milk her now while she's distracted. Don't worry, Mr Zola, she won't hurt you."

Cam handed one of the empty bottles to Bert.

"Don't let her see you coming," he said. "You take the left side and I'll take the right, and remember to be gentle. Don't move a muscle, Mr Zola."

The twins were used to milking the cows on their farm and soon both their bottles were half full. The moose still had Mr Zola pinned against the wall. She had finished licking his hat and had now turned her attention to his moustache.

"For the love of mooses, help me!" howled Mr Zola. "She's nibbling Monty."

"Nearly there," called Cam. "Just a few more squeezes."

The calf was not so happy to see its milk disappearing and started pawing the wooden floor.

"Mooaarrhh," it called, trying to nudge Bert out of the way.

"Mooaarrhh, yourself," said Bert. "There's plenty left for you, little one."

The mother moose turned at the sound of her calf and then trotted away as "God Save the Queen" started up in Mr Zola's top pocket. He pulled out the red phone with a shaking hand.

The twins stared at him. His cheese hat was covered in moose slobber, but worst of all, one half of his moustache had completely disappeared.

"Y-yes, Your Majesty," he whimpered. "I do apologize about the Crown Balloon. . . I fully understand how upset you are. . . I'm sure it can be repaired, but in the meantime, please don't concern yourself with my transport. I will find my own way of getting around. . . Yes, ma'am, the Russian police were most helpful. I'm on the Trans-Siberian Railway now . . . with some younger contestants from Cheddar Gorge. The leader, ma'am? It's early days yet, but I shall check my Cheesemaker-Locator and get back to you. . . Yes, ma'am. . . Straight away, ma'am. . . Goodbye, ma'am."

He put the phone back into his dusty man-bag and pulled out the smelling salts, inhaling deeply.

"She wants to know who the leaders are," he said, replacing the small bottle and studying the Cheesemaker-Locator attached to his wrist. "But it's hard to concentrate when one has just been manhandled by a moose!"

The twins were glad that he hadn't noticed his missing moustache yet. They peered over his shoulder, eager to find out who was in the lead. The

Cheesemaker-Locator was a large round screen with a map of the world on it. With a tap of Mr Zola's finger it zoomed in on Siberia. The twins could just make out several flashing dots. Mr Zola then scrolled down to where a flashing dot was heading south. He zoomed in closer.

"There's a 'PM' heading towards Mongolia already," he said. "Let me just check who that is."

He tapped the screen again.

"Primula Mold."

The twins glanced anxiously at each other.

"So, she *was* heading in the right direction," sighed Cam. "She must have got the moose milk already."

"Do you know this Primula Mold?" asked Mr Zola.

"Yes, she's our neighbour," said Bert. "She sailed right over us in her yellow hot air balloon."

"I'm supposed to be keeping pace with the leaders," Mr Zola sighed. "I have to catch her up, which means heading straight for Mongolia. Unfortunately, this is an overnight train. It doesn't make a stop till tomorrow. If only we could move carriages."

"Animal transportation carriages don't have connecting doors to the rest of the train," said Cam. "We had to transport some of our cattle last year and I read all about it."

"She knows everything about everything," muttered Bert to Mr Zola.

"And the reason the windows are set so high," she continued, "is so the animals can't see out, as this might panic them. But they still need light during long journeys."

"We could always go back on to the roof," said Bert, pointing towards the hatch above them. "But the problem is getting back in again."

"I don't think I can bring myself to go back up there," said Mr Zola. "We'll just have to bed down in the hay and go our separate ways in the morning. You two must form a human barrier between me and the beasts. It's the least you can do after the trauma you've put me through."

Bert looked over to the far corner of the carriage,

where the two moose were drinking from the large bucket. He slowly walked over and began to stroke the baby's fuzzy muzzle. Cam followed.

"How are we going to get to Mongolia from here?" whispered Bert.

"I thought you wanted to split up when we reached Russia," said Cam.

Bert frowned. "It might be better to do it when we reach Mongolia," he muttered. "I'm still going to win, though."

Cam nodded. "Me too," she said. "But at the moment, I think our best bet is to keep in with Mr Zola. Come on."

They wandered back to Mr Zola and sank into the hay in front of him.

"We'll make sure the moose don't come anywhere near you or Monty," said Bert, grinning. "We don't want any more *hairy* situations."

Cam glared at Bert, but Mr Zola didn't seem to notice and settled back into the hay.

"So, have you always been a cheesemaker?" asked Cam, trying to keep his attention away from his missing moustache.

"I wanted to serve my queen and country from a very young age. So I joined the Royal Air Force," said Mr Zola. "Now, that's an organization that appreciates a fine piece of nose hair! Monty and I became members of the RAF Whisker Club – a fraternal society that promotes charitable work and aid to our facially fuzzy friends. Unfortunately, it turned out that Monty didn't like heights, and we had to leave the RAF. So I decided to follow in my father's footsteps, and took up the art of cheesemaking instead. There must be something in the blood, because I'm really rather good at it."

"I am too," said Bert.

"Nearly as good as me," added Cam. "But our Gramps is the best. I wonder if he won 'Best Cheese in Show' at the fair."

"Apparently it was cancelled," said Mr Zola, closing his eyes and snuggling deeper into the hay. "Not enough entrants. Everybody was more concerned with making moose cheese, and I can't say I blame them."

Cam sighed. Gramps had been relying on winning that competition to boost their international sales. She moved closer to Bert. He was fiddling intently with a piece of straw.

"Poor Gramps," Bert whispered, glancing over to make sure Mr Zola wasn't listening. "First of all, we go off without telling him, and then 'Best Cheese in Show' is cancelled. He will not be happy."

"I know," Cam said in a low voice. "But imagine if we didn't go. There would be no hope of saving the farm. At least one of us has the chance of getting that prize money now. It's just made me more determined than ever."

Bert nodded. "And Lord Curd of Whey Farm does have a certain ring to it."

Cam snorted and fell back in the hay.

"Not as good as *Lady* Curd," she muttered.

# The Whirlwind
## (Four days to go. . .)

The following mornin a blood-curdling scream echoed the length of the Trans-Siberian train, rattling all the windows on every carriage.

"NNNNNNNNNNOOOOOOOOOOOOOO!!!!!"

Bert's eyes flew open. Mr Zola was staring into his hand mirror and screaming. Cam got up and put her arm around him.

"Don't be upset," she said. "The other half of Monty will soon grow back."

"Why Monty?" he howled. "Why didn't that

103

wretched beast take me instead? Where is the monster?"

He glanced towards the back of the carriage to where the moose was resting against a wall, its baby asleep on the floor.

"If that beast comes anywhere near me, I will not be responsible for my actions. I have a man-bag and I'm not afraid to use it."

Bert picked up a long rope from the floor and gently looped the two moose together. He secured the rope to a metal ring on the floor.

"There," he said. "As long as you stay in the far corner then the moose can't reach you. So no more talk about slapping it with your handbag."

"It's a man-bag," sniffed Mr Zola. "And I will only use it in self-defence."

He looked in the mirror again and began to make a strange agitated humming noise.

Cam patted him on the back. She didn't like seeing anyone distressed and felt slightly responsible. They had used the Monty-munching incident to get their moose milk.

"I think half a moustache suits you," she said. "It's different – unique. You could start a new fashion."

Mr Zola fiddled with the hairy remnants.

"Do you really think so?" he asked, staring searchingly into the mirror.

"Absolutely!" said Cam, straightening his hat, which was covered in moosey saliva and hay. "You're looking good. And before you know it, the other half of your moustache will have grown back bigger and bushier than before."

Mr Zola continued to gaze into the mirror.

"And you know what they say," added Bert. "It's no use crying over spilled moustaches . . . or even nibbled moustaches."

"I've never heard that saying before," murmured Mr Zola, "but I shall try and soldier on. It's what Monty would have wanted."

"That's the spirit," said Cam. "Now, let's try and put this behind us and get back to business. What's the quickest way to Mongolia? We've only got four days left until the State Banquet."

"*We?*" repeated Mr Zola, getting to his feet. "I'm afraid there is no *we*."

Cam bit her bottom lip.

A loud thud from outside shook the carriage and interrupted her thoughts. Mr Zola stood on a hay bale and looked out of one of the small windows.

"We've just been hit by a tree!" he shouted. "There's a Siberian storm raging out there."

Another crash rocked the carriage, disturbing the moose. The mother grunted and moved protectively over her calf.

"That was a branch!" cried Mr Zola. "There's an enormous whirlwind passing right overhead."

"Thank goodness we're not on the roof now," said Cam. "Are we nearly there?"

"We're approaching the city of Krasnoyarsk," he said, still staring out of the window.

"A city?" repeated Cam. "I thought Siberia was just a snowy wilderness."

"A lot of it is," said Mr Zola. "But there are several large cities too. We're just about to cross the

Krasnoyarsk Bridge, a prime example of a parabolic polygonal truss bridge."

"Is he talking Russian again?" asked Bert.

"It crosses the Yenisey River, which flows all the way down to the Arctic Ocean in Siberia the Khangai Mountains of Mongolia," continued Mr Zola. "My research into moose-cheese ingredients has left me with a good knowledge of this region. The train will cross the bridge and pull into the station, where I will be purchasing a first-class ticket on a boat down the Yenisey."

"What will we do?" asked Cam.

"You'll have to find your own way to Mongolia," replied Mr Zola. "I am not a babysitter. My priority is catching up with this Primula Mold."

"That's ours too," said Bert.

"You've managed to tag along with me this far," grumbled Mr Zola. "And you've caused me nothing but trouble. I shall be glad of some adult company. However, should you take the lead in the competition, then I'm sure we shall meet again. Although thankfully, I think that's pretty unlikely."

"Why?" demanded Bert.

"You're just children! You were very lucky to get the moose milk but I doubt very much that you will get any rennet. You probably don't even know what it is."

"It's the chemical found in mammals' stomachs," said Cam. "It curdles the milk and is an essential ingredient in cheese production."

"Know-all," he muttered.

"Told you," said Bert.

"Anyway," continued Mr Zola, "it's time for us to part company."

As he spoke, something else crashed against the carriage, and the train began to brake. Mr Zola looked out of the window again.

"Good gracious!" he cried. "That was a rubber boat. The whirlwind is flinging all manner of things up from the city. And there goes a tent! The train driver's going to have to be extra careful crossing the bridge. The wind is extremely strong up here."

There was a rhythmic clatter as the train slowed to a walking pace. They could hear the wind howling outside. Bert jumped up and down on the hay bale, trying to see out of the high window.

"Give me a leg up, Cam," he said. "I want to see a Siberian whirlwind."

"All right, but my turn next."

Bert clambered on to his sister's back and looked out of the window. The view was amazing. The Krasnoyarsk Bridge was a symmetrical tangle of intricate ironwork, its main frame curving over the river like a metal rainbow. A large city rose up on the other side, the roofs covered in a thick layer of snow. Fifty metres below the bridge streams of water snaked through the ice. A small ship with a large round hull was forging through the frozen water.

"Look! An icebreaker," shouted Bert.

But it was the whirlwind tossing things into the air that amazed him the most. He watched as an inflatable tyre, a small shed and even a red bouncy castle were flung around the sky like matchsticks.

"My turn," said Cam. "I want to see."

Bert reluctantly climbed down.

"I haven't finished looking yet," he said. "If we could just open the outside door a little, then we'll both see. And I could do with some fresh air. It smells a bit moosey in here."

"No!" cried Mr Zola. "There's a huge whirlwind out there, you idiot! We would be blown out of the train!"

But Bert had already unbolted the huge gate and started to slide it back. A tunnel of icy wind roared into the carriage, smashing into the walls and hurling everyone off their feet. Bert made a frantic grab for his sister just as they were all sucked out of the train.

# 12

## The Bouncy Castle

Cam and Bert were wrenched apart and whipped up into the Siberian sky like crumbs in a vacuum cleaner. Cam lost all sense of her surroundings as the whirlwind sucked the air from her lungs and pounded her face with tiny ice particles. She felt herself being tossed round and round as it roared over the bridge and out on to the river.

Bert managed to catch a breath as the fierce wind eventually lost some of its momentum. He could feel his ears popping as the pressure dropped, and he opened his eyes as the wind died completely.

Cam was right beside him, floating in mid-air like a piece of litter blown up in the storm. There was a second of calm before they both dropped like stones, hurtling towards the frozen river below. Bert could hear Cam shrieking, but her scream was drowned out by a much louder one, as Mr Zola tumbled past. Bert reached out for his sister and they managed to link fingers. But just as he thought they would crash into the ice, Mr Zola reappeared in front of them, soaring back up again and still screaming loudly. Bert glanced down just in time to see a mound of red rubber beneath them. There was a loud BOING as the twins fell into the object. Cam hit a wobbling wall and was boosted sideways, knocking into Bert, who bounced into a returning Mr Zola. Eventually, the three of them lay in a rippling heap in the middle of the billowing rubber.

"I don't believe it!" cried Bert. "We've landed on that bouncy castle we saw flying through the air! It must have blown on to the river. Is everyone OK?"

They lay on their backs, panting heavily.

"I think so," groaned Cam. "But that was terrifying. I thought we were going to die."

Mr Zola stared fearfully up into the sky. "It's not too late," he mumbled. "What about the moose? They could come raining down on us at any moment."

"They'll be safe," said Bert. "I secured them to the carriage, remember? It probably saved their lives."

Mr Zola tried to get to his feet but the wind picked up again, hitting the back of the bouncy castle and propelling it along the frozen river. He fell back and almost bounced right out.

"We're going to take off again," he whimpered, grasping hold of one of the large rubber air-plugs attached to the floor. "This is all your fault! Monty is traumatized and I've lost my cheese hat!"

The weight of the two children and Mr Zola kept the bouncy castle from being tossed into the air again. But it sped along the ice at breakneck speed, leaving the Krasnoyarsk Bridge far behind.

"Hold on to one of those plugs," called Bert to Cam. "But be careful you don't disturb the seal. We don't want to lose any air. This is going to be a fast ride."

After a little while Cam let go and bounced over to a wobbly wall.

"Actually, this isn't too bad," she said, looking out on to the river. "Look how far we've gone already."

Bert joined her as the bouncy castle hurtled past an icebreaking ship. He waved to the astonished people on board.

"We're much faster than them," he said. "It's brilliant!"

"Brilliant?" yelped Mr Zola, clinging to his air-plug. "It's intolerable!"

"We should be grateful," said Cam. "This bouncy castle saved our lives. What on earth was it doing blowing around?"

"I guess Siberian kids have birthday parties too," replied Bert. "But what are we going to do when the wind dies down?"

But the wind didn't die down, and for the rest of the day they sat back for the ride and watched as the pine forests of Siberia gave way to tracts of wilderness with remote villages nestled on the banks. Children dressed in bright colours ran out of their houses, pointing and waving as the castle whizzed by.

"Bouncy castles really are the only way to travel," said Cam, leaning over the back wall. She almost toppled over and was hauled back by Bert.

"Careful," he said. "If you fall out, there's no turning this thing around."

"I'm OK," she said. But she still hung on to Bert as she peeped over the wall.

"Look! What's going on over there on the far bank?"

A man with red hair was standing on top of a trailer attached to the back of a car. He was surveying the surrounding area with a pair of binoculars.

"It's Gramps' friend Lester," shouted Bert. "Mr Lester, over here. Over here!"

The man swivelled round and fixed them with his binoculars.

"Bert?" he yelled. "Cam? Is that you?"

"Yes. We're on our way to Mongolia," shouted Bert. "How about you?"

"Moose stalking," cried Lester. "Have you found one yet?"

Bert proudly held up his bottle of milk.

"How did you get that?" shouted Lester in disbelief.

"You've got to have nous to get the moose juice!" called Bert.

The twins grinned and waved goodbye to the astonished man as the castle whooshed by.

"Well, at least we're not last," said Cam. "Has anyone got anything to eat? I'm starving."

Bert reached into his pocket and threw her a large brown lump.

"What is it?"

"Moose biscuits," said Bert. "I found them on the train. Thought they might come in handy. Do you want one, Mr Zola?"

"I would rather starve than munch on a moose morsel," he said, turning up his nose.

"Suit yourself," said Bert, bouncing up on to the back wall. "Hey! There's someone following us down the river. It looks like a couple of speed skaters."

Mr Zola was too scared to bounce up and look but Cam stood on tiptoe and peeked over the wall. Sure enough, two figures were skating in single file, both bent low over the ice and taking huge strides. They flew along the frozen water.

"They're catching us up!" cried Cam. "I think it's a couple of bears!"

Mr Zola looked up.

"Are you telling me that we are being approached by two speed-skating bears?" he asked. "What's in those moose biscuits?"

The skaters were nearly level with the castle.

"They do look quite furry," said Bert, "and they're chanting something."

The two figures saluted Cam and Bert as they zoomed past the bouncy castle, their long embroidered ears waving in the wind.

"Moose cheese! Moose cheese! Moose cheese!"

"It's the Easy Cheesy Doggy Treats Society!" shouted Cam.

"And they're beating us!" yelled Bert. "We have to go faster."

"We can't. We're reliant on the wind."

"Typical!" muttered Mr Zola, checking his Cheesemaker-Locator. "I'm supposed to be keeping abreast of the leaders in this competition, and instead I'm stuck in a bouncy castle with a couple of cheddar-urchins. According to my radar, Primula Mold is already in Mongolia. The Easy Cheesy men are just in front of us and the Specialist Cheesemakers Association are right behind, heading south. Everyone else is still in Siberia."

"God Save the Queen" struck up in Mr Zola's top pocket. He pulled out the red phone.

"It's her again," he said. "This time I'm prepared. . . Your Majesty. . . I am, as we speak, heading down the Yenisey River towards Mongolia. An icebreaker, ma'am? . . . No, not exactly . . . more of an ice-bouncer. . . It's complicated, ma'am. . . However, several contestants have obtained Siberian moose milk, and are now heading to Mongolia. . . Yes, ma'am? . . . A yak festival, you say? . . . Of course, ma'am. . . On my way now."

Mr Zola replaced the phone. "It would appear that the nomadic tribes of northern Mongolia are holding a traditional yak festival on the plains at the foot of the Khangai Mountains," he said. "This area has the highest concentration of yaks in the world. Her Majesty believes it will be a good source for yak rennet, and I'm sure that is where our furry friends from the Easy Cheesy Doggy Treats Society are heading right now."

"What exactly is a yak festival?" asked Bert

"It's a Mongolian version of the World Cheese Fair," said Mr Zola. "There will be yak competitions and events, some games, and hopefully lots of food stalls. I'm extremely hungry."

Bert pulled out another moose biscuit. "Sure I can't tempt you?" he asked. "They fill you up."

Mr Zola wrinkled his nose but held out his hand and accepted the biscuit.

"It smells like dried dung," he said, sniffing the

brown lump before popping it into his mouth. "And tastes like it too."

As they travelled further south, the snow on the trees began to disappear and they could hear loud cracking sounds as the ice on the river started to melt.

"We're slowing down," said Bert. "The wind is dying off. We're never going to catch the Easy Cheesy Doggy Treats men now."

Mr Zola released his grasp on the rubber plug and stood up. "I wonder where we are?" he said, checking his radar.

The sun was just beginning to set behind a large group of mountains in the far distance.

"I think they're the Khangai Mountains," he said. "The wind has stopped but the ice is melting and the current of the river should carry us along. Thankfully, the castle sides are high enough to keep the water out. We will be in Mongolia by morning."

The twins started bouncing up and down in excitement, shooting Mr Zola high in the air.

"Careful!" he shouted. "Monty's still recovering from a nasty shock."

The twins laughed and carried on bouncing.

"You're like a couple of demented pogo sticks," scowled Mr Zola. "Come and settle down in a corner. Try and get some sleep. The ice has nearly melted and as long as we don't spring a leak, we should float along the river all night."

The twins did as they were told, and wedged themselves in between the wall and the bottom of the castle. They pulled their coats tightly around them, glad that they had left the bitter winds of Siberia far behind and blissfully unaware that they were heading towards one of the largest dams in the world.

# 13

## The Dam Dive
### (Three days to go. . .)

The next day dawned bright and clear. The bouncy castle was floating in a calm lake with the sun just beginning to peep over a ragged mountain. Mr Zola was lying flat on his back in the middle of the bouncy castle, murmuring gently in his sleep.

"Monty, I love you. . ."

Bert nudged Cam and pointed to the mumbling Mr Zola. She began to giggle as Bert knelt down beside him.

"Monty, I want to marry you," he whispered in

Mr Zola's ear.

Cam burst out laughing and Mr Zola's eyes pinged open. He sat up sharply and glared at Bert.

"How dare you suggest things to Monty whilst I'm sleeping," he grumbled.

"Sorry!" chuckled Bert. "Don't be angry. Here, have a moose biscuit."

Mr Zola grudgingly took the biscuit. "Woken up by a cheddar-urchin with a dung biscuit," he sighed. "On the positive side, I think those must be the Khangai Mountains. I have single-handedly navigated the mighty Yenisey River and brought us safely to Mongolia."

"What are you talking about?" said Bert. "All you did was cling to the side like a soggy lettuce leaf!"

Mr Zola pretended not to hear and looked out at the view.

The river stretched out behind them. The lake was sandwiched between two rocky mountains which rose up sharply either side. The castle was drifting backwards.

"We need to turn the castle around," said Cam.

"To see where we're going."

There was a gentle bump and the bouncy castle came to a complete standstill.

"We've hit something," said Bert, trying to look over the back wall. "I can't see anything. It's just space."

"What do you mean, *it's just space*?" asked Mr Zola. "It can't be."

"If we all run round in a circle, it should rotate the castle," said Cam. "C'mon. I'll chase Bert, and Bert chases Mr Zola, and Mr Zola chases me."

The three of them began running round the outside of the castle close to the walls. It slowly began to turn in a complete circle. Mr Zola fell into the middle.

"I can't do it any more," he said. "Monty's too dizzy."

The twins joined him and they all sat down, watching as the castle slowly rotated, revealing the top edge of a huge dam.

A giant slope of grey concrete fell away beneath them, vertically at first, then curving gently out to meet a fast-flowing, bubbling river below. The tip of a wall poked out of the water in front of the castle, just about preventing them from sliding over the top.

Bert's heart felt like it was doing a little drum roll inside his rib cage.

"Does this thing come with seat belts?" he joked. But his voice sounded high and unnatural.

Cam swallowed deeply and looked over the edge. This was all her fault. She had forged the letter from Gramps and now they were in terrible trouble – again.

"Try not to make any sudden movements," she breathed. "We're going to have to try and paddle very gently to the far bank. Are you ready, Mr Zola . . . Mr Zola? Are you all right?

Mr Zola had buried his head into the soft rubber of the bouncy castle. "We're all going to die," he wailed. "It's not fair! I can't take any more!" He began pummelling his hands and feet against the floor.

"I don't want to be balancing on the edge of a colossal dam in a bouncy castle with soggy smelling salts!" he yelled, pulling the bottle from his battered man-bag and tossing it over the edge of the dam. "Soggy smelling salts are about as useful as half a moustache!"

The twins looked at each other in alarm. Cam reached over and took his hand.

"Mr Zola, you must try to keep still!"

"He's finally lost it," said Bert.

"Lost it?" repeated Mr Zola. "Lost it? OF COURSE I'VE LOST IT! I've lost the Crown Balloon, half a moustache, my smelling salts, my cheese hat, and my. . ."

"Mind!"

"Shush, Bert! Mr Zola, you need to calm down. You're wobbling the castle over the edge of the dam."

Mr Zola's pummelling had bounced the lip of the castle over the top of the wall.

"I don't care!" he screamed, beating his hands down like a toddler. "I don't care about anything any more!"

The castle bounced forward and teetered on the edge of the dam. Half of it was on the water, half of it dangling in space. It slowly began to tip.

"WE'RE GOING!" shrieked Cam.

"HANG ON TO SOMETHING!" shouted Bert, diving on to one of the rubber air-plugs. Cam grabbed hold of her brother as Mr Zola grasped the other plug.

The bouncy castle did a final see-saw before tipping ninety degrees and plunging vertically down the smooth concrete. Cam's long hair flew out behind her and she gasped for breath as her stomach flipped. She closed her eyes and clung on to the back of Bert's coat. She could hear Mr Zola screeching in terror and Bert whooping excitedly. Finally, the concrete wall began to curve round and level out. The castle shot off the end of the dam wall and continued whizzing across the top of the bubbling water.

"We've made it!" she yelled.

"Not quite," shouted Bert. "Don't let go!"

The force of their descent propelled them down the white rapids. The river coursed through huge boulders, knocking the bouncy castle from one bank to the other. Cam could hear the water getting louder in front of them.

"WATERFALL!" she screamed, as they crashed down a sharp slope of water.

The bouncy castle ricocheted off a rock, hitting a jagged tree trunk protruding from the riverbank. There was a loud BANG as it gouged a large hole in the side. The castle took off as the air from inside gushed out. The twins were flung out on to the bank unharmed, but Mr Zola remained clinging to the castle. The loudest raspberry noise filled the valley as the bouncy castle whizzed around the air like a popped balloon.

TTTTTHHHHHHHHHBBBBBBBBBLLL-LUUUUUGGGGGGHHHHHHHHHHHHHH

"THAT WASN'T ME!" shrieked Mr Zola, as he flew over the twins' heads, his body jerking from side to side as the deflating castle spiralled out of sight.

# 14

## The Yak Festival

The twins scrambled down the side of the mountain, following the distant raspberry noise and faint screams of "Help!" They just caught sight of the deflated bouncy castle with Mr Zola still clinging to it, making a final skyward soar before dropping in between a group of large round tents in the middle of a vast grassy plain. Cam and Bert staggered towards them as fast as they could.

"Poor Mr Zola," panted Cam. "I hope he's OK. I don't think he can take much more."

"I'm not sure I can either," moaned Bert. "That might have been the best water slide ever, but I'm exhausted. I need something to eat other than moose biscuits."

As they got closer they could see that the tents were surrounded by enormous holding pens full of huge hairy cows with large curved horns.

"Buffalo!" shouted Bert.

"They're yaks, you dummy," said Cam. "This must be the festival."

Several people dressed in brightly coloured robes had surrounded the flattened bouncy castle. As the twins approached, they could hear "God Save the Queen" begin to play from beneath the shrivelled pile of rubber. Bert pushed through the crowd and pulled back a deflated wall, revealing a crumpled Mr Zola beneath. The remaining half of Monty was stuck to the right side of his cheek like a squashed spider and his dusty hair was poking out in random tufts. He pulled out the red phone with a trembling hand.

"Your Majesty," he croaked. ". . . Yes, I got

here eventually, ma'am . . . dam trouble. . . No, I'm not swearing . . . I flew the last part. . . Yes, it was extremely fast . . . the leader? Primula Mold, ma'am. . . Not yet, ma'am. . . I will, ma'am. . . Of course, ma'am . . . straight away, ma'am."

He put the phone back and stared blankly ahead of him. Cam and Bert grabbed his hands and pulled him to his feet.

"Are you OK?" asked Bert.

"Yes, ma'am," mumbled Mr Zola.

"I'm not the Queen!"

"No, ma'am."

Cam looked around at the astonished crowd surrounding them. "Can somebody help us?" she asked. "I think our friend has had a knock to the head."

A lady dressed in a green robe and a fur-trimmed hat came forward.

"*Sain baina uu,*" she said, smiling.

"That's the problem," said Bert, pointing to Mr Zola. "He's not sane. In fact, he's completely insane – nuttier than a vegetarian roast dinner, loopier than a hula hoop, madder than a—"

"*Sain baina uu* means 'hello'," she interrupted. "Come and rest in my yurt. You *all* look a little crazy."

Cam glanced across at Bert. His face was filthy and his jacket was ripped in several places. His fair hair had turned a muddy brown and was sticking up in large clumps. She put her hand up to her own hair. Half of it was bundled on top of her head in a thick matted lump. She pulled out a long piece of grass.

"We've been travelling a long way," she explained. "We're very tired and hungry."

The lady nodded and led them to a large round tent. It was similar to one of the marquees at home, with a pole in the middle holding up the main frame. The floor was covered in thick rugs with large cushions scattered on top. To one side was a small cooking stove with a pot bubbling on the top.

"My name is Saran," she said, as they all sank on to the soft cushions. "This is my yurt. I sell things made from yak hair – cushions, rugs and bags mainly."

"I'm sorry but we haven't got any money," sighed Cam.

"I don't want to sell you anything," said Saran. "You look exhausted, poor children. You need to rest. Would you like some soup?"

Cam and Bert nodded enthusiastically.

"You're very kind," said Bert.

She smiled and ladled out two bowls of steaming noodle soup from the pot.

"I have plenty," she said, handing them the bowls with a large slice of pitta bread. "What about your friend?"

Mr Zola was staring into space, muttering under his breath.

"He's had a nasty shock – lost half his moustache, amongst other things," mumbled Cam through a mouthful of bread. "Do you have any smelling salts?"

"I don't. But I could fix his moustache."

Mr Zola blinked and turned to face Saran. "What did you say?"

"That's if you want a whole one," she said. "I have

133

the softest black yak hair that I could weave into the other half. It would make a fine moustache."

Mr Zola smiled broadly. "I suddenly feel much better," he said, propping himself up. "You're a lifesaver, dear lady. But I must insist on paying. I have some Mongolian currency in case of an emergency such as this."

Saran smiled and pulled a clump of black yak hair from a large knitted bag. "Many westerners visit our festival," she said, teasing the fibres apart. "You have strange customs. Today I meet a man with half a moustache. . ."

Mr Zola brought his hand up and shielded Monty protectively.

". . .and earlier I met an old lady with a mouldy cheese around her neck."

Bert nearly choked on his soup. "Primula Mold!" he coughed.

Mr Zola checked his Cheesemaker-Locator.

"According to this, she's now heading west towards Kazakhstan," he sighed. "I'm never going to catch her up."

"She won a yak race and left," said Saran. "She was very good for her age. Very strong."

"Very strong smelling," muttered Bert. "Fancy Primula Mold racing a yak. I wonder why?"

"She wanted the prize, of course," said Saran. "All our winners receive the rarest delicacy produced by a yak – rennet from the fourth stomach."

The twins looked at each other in dismay, their hearts sinking.

"How do you get to race a yak?" asked Bert.

"There's a race starting soon," said Saran. "Why don't you watch while I finish your friend's moustache?"

The twins finished their soup and washed their faces and hands in a bowl of warm soapy water that Saran gave them. Cam brushed her hair and tied it back with twine made of yak hair. They left Mr Zola with Saran and walked out into the festival feeling much better. Colourful flags were strung from tent to tent and wound around the holding pens full of yaks.

"I wonder where we go to watch the yak races?" said Cam.

"There's no point just watching," snorted Bert. "I'm going to see if I can take part in the next race."

"Not without me!"

They walked through the crowded stalls. It was very busy. Huge pots of vegetable soups and mutton stews bubbled on large cooking stoves. Children ran past with paper bags overflowing with little round balls of cheese.

"I wish we had some money," said Bert. "I could murder a cheese ball."

They passed a small white tent and peered in. It was full of shelves, each one packed with round clay pots. A man in a purple pointed hat beckoned them in.

"Rennet for sale," he said. "All types of rennet."

The twin's eyes widened.

"Do you sell rennet from the fourth stomach of a yak?" asked Bert.

The man laughed loudly, his deep voice resonating through the small tent. "I have just been asked that by two men dressed as dogs," he said.

"And before that, by an old woman with a strange medallion."

Bert and Cam swapped an ominous look.

"Rennet from the fourth stomach is the most precious of ingredients because it doesn't occur in normal yaks," continued the man, "only from the rare albino yak of Outer Mongolia. Some say it has magical healing properties. Others believe that one mouthful will bring you good fortune for the rest of your life. But you cannot buy it –You have to achieve it. I have other yak rennet if you're interested. This one is from the first stomach – perfect for a fuller flavoured cheese. This one is from the second – low in fat and mild in taste. And this one. . ." He held up a red pot with a black skull and crossbones on the label. "This one is from the third stomach. Highly dangerous, but perfect for poisoning unwanted rodents."

"You use it to make poisoned cheese to kill rats?" asked Bert. "That's a bit unfair."

"Not when the rats are nibbling your yak cheese!"

"The only rennet we need is from the fourth stomach," said Cam.

"Then you must find Attila," said the man. "And race one of his yaks to victory. You will find him in the blue yurt with the gold trim next to the largest of the yak pens."

They left the small tent and looked around for the blue yurt. They walked past a wrestling competition. Two men dressed in nothing but red pants, blue sleeves, boots and round hats with a small tower on top were locked together, furiously trying to push the other to the ground. Bert asked if he could have a go but then decided he didn't want to reveal his pants to the surrounding crowd.

They skirted round an archery competition. Ten men and women in gold and crimson robes were standing with their feet astride and their bows held up to their faces. The targets were so far away, Cam and Bert could hardly see them. They wanted to stop and watch but knowing Primula Mold was ahead of them meant they had to hurry on.

Eventually they came to a large pen filled with yaks of every size and shape. A giant of a man in plain brown robes and with a plaited black beard was inside the pen patting the yaks and checking their horns and hooves. Bert climbed up on to the side fence and was immediately surrounded by several yaks all mooing gently and snuffling against him. The man looked up and watched as Bert stroked their large hairy ears and talked gently to them.

"*Sain baina uu,*" called the man.

"Soon boona ee," said Bert, feeling slightly embarrassed at his first attempt at speaking Mongolian. "We're looking for a man called Attila. Do you know where we can find him?"

"You just have," he said, bowing low.

Bert bowed back. "My name is Bert Curd and this is my sister, Cam," he said. "The man in the rennet tent said I might be able to race one of your yaks. I need to win some special rennet."

"Me too," murmured Cam, shyly.

Attila pushed his way through his animals and sat on the side of the pen next to Bert.

"Are you experienced yak racers?" he asked.

"Back home we have cows," said Cam.

"Yes, we love cow racing," added Bert, turning slightly pink. "Do it all the time. The cow sprint, the cow cross-country, the cow sack race. My particular favourite is the cow seven-legged race. When you tie the legs of two cows together and—"

"All right, Bert," whispered Cam. "You're overdoing it."

They both looked up hopefully at Attila.

"How much will you pay?" he asked.

"Four moose biscuits," said Bert, feeling around in his pockets.

Attila gave a great snort of laughter and jumped back into the pen. "I'm afraid that is not enough, young man. My yaks are all very precious to me."

"Four moose biscuits and a conker?" asked Bert, digging deeper in his pocket.

Attila's rich laugh filled the pen. "I admire your spirit," he said, patting a particularly large yak. "But Genghis here doesn't eat moose biscuits or conkers."

"I think Genghis prefers eating children," whispered Bert, looking up at the huge beast.

"What if we share the prize with you?" asked Cam, jumping up on to the fence. "We'll give you half the special rennet."

Attila stopped laughing and nodded slowly. "And if you don't win?" he asked.

"I will win," she said. "I have to. But when Bert loses, he can muck out the yak pen for you."

"Hey!" cried Bert. "I can beat you with my eyes closed. Even if I had the tiniest yak, I could outrun you."

"You wish! I'm going to leave you standing!"

"Yeah – standing at the finish line waiting for you!"

Attila made his way back to the twins. "I can see how determined you are to beat each other," he said, "but there will be others in the race. How will you defeat them?"

"You don't understand how much is resting on this race," said Cam. "I have to win that rennet."

"So do I," cried Bert, "and I'm going to."

Attila looked from one twin to the other. "You are bold – I like that," he said, holding out his hand.

"It's a deal. With twins, I have two chances of winning."

"How did you know we were twins?" asked Bert. "We don't look anything like each other."

Attila laughed. "If you say so," he said. "But if either of you win, then you give me half the rennet, and if you lose, then you will both be shovelling yak pats."

He turned and began to look for two suitable animals for the twins.

"I am so gonna win," said Bert. "How hard can it be? The yaks do all the running, all I have to do is hold on."

Attila led Genghis out of the pen and handed his rope to Bert.

"I think he might suit you," said Attila. "Genghis is fast and courageous."

Next Attila led out a slightly smaller animal and walked it over to Cam.

"And I think you will connect well with Zogs," he said. "She is a clever animal who knows exactly what she wants. Climb up and I'll lead you to the start. A race is just about to begin."

The twins clambered up the side of the pen and mounted their yaks. Bert was at least a head higher than Cam. Neither of them had ever ridden a cow, let alone a yak. They both gripped the animals' shaggy manes tightly, their hearts hammering with excitement.

# 15

## Yak Racing

"Hello down there," called Bert from his enormous yak. "This beast is going to blow you away."

"He might be big," answered Cam, "but Zogs is clever. She will find a way to win."

"You don't stand a chance. Genghis and I have connected."

"That's because you both have yak brains," grinned Cam.

Attila led them through the festival to the start of the race. Bert let go of Genghis's long hair and began waving at the crowds.

"As Lord Curd mounts his trusty steed," he said, "his loyal fans gather, eager to see a true master of the yak race—"

Genghis sneezed and Bert slipped, tumbling forward over the yak's dipped head. The crowd laughed and Cam giggled as Attila picked him up and helped him back on. Bert scowled and held on tightly to Genghis's shaggy mane.

A line of flags marked the start. Attila explained they had to race along the grassy plain towards a star-shaped rock in the distance.

"You must gallop around the rock-star and back towards the start. First across the line of flags will receive the pot of rennet from the fourth stomach. I will be watching you with interest."

They lined up with the rest of the competitors. They weren't the only children. Two Mongolian boys and a girl of about the same age were crouching over their yaks, focusing on the rock ahead. There were several other people dressed in colourful robes and at the far end three men all in white suits and white sunglasses.

"Look!" cried Cam. "It's the men from the Specialist Cheesemakers Association. They must have got the moose milk."

"So we're not just racing against each other," said Bert, "and look who else just turned up."

Cam turned to see the two Easy Cheesy Doggy Treats men. Their yaks were tiny and it was hard to see where the yak ended and the men in their doggy outfits started. As they lined up next to the children the twins could hear them chanting.

"Moose cheese, moose cheese, moose cheese. . ."

A tall man in a yak-hair hat stood at the end of the line and held up a large gong. Cam bent low over Zogs, holding tightly with her hands and knees. She glanced over at Bert, who was sitting up high and holding on with one hand.

DONG!

The gong donged and the yaks jumped into action.

"YEEHAA!" cried Bert.

He was almost thrown off as Genghis exploded forward, propelling him backwards. Cam closed her eyes and clung to Zogs' thick hair as the yak broke into a run. Her body bounced furiously up and down and she bent lower still, so that her head was resting on Zogs' neck. She could hear the pounding of hooves all around her and briefly opened her eyes to see one of the men in white suits hammer past.

"C'mon, Zogs!" she called, squeezing her knees tighter.

The yak sped up and Cam could see they had left several competitors behind, including both the Easy Cheesy Doggy Treats men and two of the Specialist Cheesemakers. She heard Bert shouting in front of her.

"Ride 'em, yakboy," he yelled, as they raced up to the rock-star.

One of the other boys in the race reached the rock first, closely followed by the girl and one of the Specialist Cheesemakers. Bert was close on their heels, with Cam just behind him. As Zogs galloped around the bend, Cam began slipping sideways. She gripped tighter with her knees but that just made the yak go faster and she slid down further. Zogs caught up with Genghis. Bert glanced over as they thundered past.

"Hey!" shouted Bert. "You're not allowed to ride them sideways."

"I am not doing this on purpose!" screamed Cam as they zoomed ahead.

She managed to pull herself up on to Zogs' back again and glanced behind at Bert. Genghis had slowed right down to a trot. Eventually he stopped to eat a particularly large clump of grass. Bert was desperately trying to urge him on.

"What do you think you're doing?" he shouted in frustration. "No wonder you're so beefy!"

Genghis completely ignored him and continued munching.

Cam and Zogs galloped towards the line of flags in the distance. She saw one of the Easy Cheesy Doggy Treats men still heading the other way towards the rock-star. He had given up trying to ride his tiny yak and was now sprinting forward, carrying it on his back. The yak seemed undisturbed and was nibbling on one of his long embroidered ears.

She could see the others ahead of her and dug her knees in even tighter. Zogs pounded towards them, throwing Cam from side to side. She lost her hold and began sliding down again until she was completely under the yak. She gripped the long hair with all her might as the ground beneath flew past.

From her upside-down position she could see Bert and Genghis far behind. Genghis was now following one of the other yaks and was mooing amorously at it.

"This is no time for romance!" yelled Bert.

Cam clung to Zogs' belly like a baby monkey. She didn't know how long she could hold on like this or how far the finish line was. The tighter she gripped, the faster Zogs went, and soon they had overtaken everyone except the Specialist Cheesemaker in white.

"Faster, Zogs!" she shouted. "We can't let him win."

Zogs seemed to respond, but just as they were level with them, Cam felt the bottle of moose milk in her pocket come loose. But she couldn't let go of the speeding yak, and as they crossed the finish line to great cheers, the bottle fell from her coat and smashed into the hard ground, splashing the precious moose milk everywhere.

# 16

## Trek to Kazakhstan

Cam had won the yak race. Attila caught hold of Zogs and she let go of the yak's hairy belly and rolled out from under its hooves. He pulled Cam to her feet and held her arm up and shouted something in Mongolian. The surrounding crowd started cheering wildly. The man in white from the Specialist Cheese Association scowled at her as he climbed down from his yak. She had beaten him by a horn. The other competitors came trotting in. Bert was second to last, followed by the Easy Cheesy Doggy Treats man, who was still carrying his yak on his back. One ear of his doggy suit had been completely chewed off.

Attila lifted Cam up and sat her on his shoulders. A woman approached them wearing the Mongolian national costume – a scarlet floor-length tunic with a high collar. It was embroidered with gold and silver braid. Bright blue tassels hung down from her elaborate round hat. She held up a velvet cushion with a small ceramic pot of rennet on top. Cam accepted her prize and the crowd cheered enthusiastically.

"Well done, Cam!" cried Attila, setting her down on her feet. "You have nerves of steel. You've shown that I, Attila, own some of the fastest yaks in Mongolia."

The crowd started to disperse and Bert came shuffling over with Genghis gently pushing against him.

"OK, OK," he muttered to the yak. "I shouldn't have called you beefy, but *you* shouldn't have slowed down. Now I've lost the race to my rotten sister. She's got the rennet and I'm never going to be Lord Curd."

Genghis mooed sympathetically as Bert looked over at Cam.

"I suppose you want me to congratulate you," he said. "But there should be a rule about riding a yak upside down. It's just not fair."

Cam burst out crying. "It doesn't matter," she wailed. "I lost my moose milk. It's all gone!"

Attila put his enormous tree trunk arm around her. "Are you not happy to win?" he asked.

"I haven't won," she sobbed. "You don't understand. I can't win the Great Moose Cheese Chase without my milk. I've lost everything – the prize money, the title, our farm, my grandpa's trust – everything!"

"What is this Great Meese Chase Choose?" asked Attila.

Cam was sobbing too hard to speak.

"The Great Moose Cheese Chase," corrected Bert.

Attila listened closely as Bert told him their whole story, from Cheddar Gorge to Mongolia.

"Moose cheese!" he gasped. "For your queen?

Why didn't you tell me before? I feel honoured to be part of such a courageous quest. But surely everything is not lost, Cam. Your brother still has his moose milk and now you have the rennet."

"Are you saying we should work together?" sniffed Cam.

"Of course! The men in white suits and the men in doggy suits are working as teams. Why aren't you?"

"Because we want to beat each other," said Bert. "Prove who is the best."

Attila frowned and shook his head. "Best at what? Everyone has different strengths – use each other's to your advantage. While you are fighting, your cheesy neighbour is winning. Is that what you want?"

The twins shook their heads.

"Do you know how lucky you are?" continued Attila. "Twins have a special connection that begins before birth. You will always have somebody there for you. Family bonds are precious. Use them and you could win. If not, then it will be victory for Mouldy Prim."

"Primula Mold," giggled Cam through her tears.

"You sound like our grandpa," said Bert. "He's always going on about how special twins are."

"Then maybe you should listen to him. He sounds like a wise man."

Bert nodded. He always felt a little pang of guilt when he thought about Gramps.

"He would love it if we won this together," said Cam.

"I know," agreed Bert. "We really would be 'the incredible Curd twins' then."

"Shall we do it? For Gramps?"

"OK! Let's give it a go."

Attila smiled approvingly and watched as Zogs and Genghis nudged against the twins like two enormous cats desperate for a stroke.

"My yaks like you," he said. "I like you! I want to help with your quest. You may keep all of the rennet. I would only use it for trading. Your need is greater than mine. And if you wish, I can take you to the Kazakhstan border. My tribe is leaving the festival today and travelling west. We are nomadic and never stay longer than a few days in one place."

"Thank you," cried Cam.

"But I will take you no further than the border," said Attila. "I have heard of the deserted salt mines that you talk of. They are haunted by evil spirits and I have no wish to visit."

"Evil spirits?" repeated Bert. "The Queen never mentioned evil spirits."

"The salt mine was built on an ancient Kazakh burial ground," said Attila. "They say the tunnelling disturbed the spirits and they took their revenge. The mine collapsed into the ground over a hundred years ago but some of the shafts still remain. It is a brave person who dares to descend into the mines. I admire your courage."

"Thanks," said Cam. She didn't feel very courageous. If someone as big and bold as Attila was too scared to enter the mines, how would they ever manage it?

Attila led the twins and the animals back through the festival towards the yak pen. They saw Mr Zola emerging from the rennet tent. His new moustache was about twice the size of his old one. He had obviously had both sides done, as it now curled round in a thick symmetrical bush, covering his entire upper lip and most of his cheeks. He was studying a small red pot.

"Mr Zola," called Cam. "I won a yak race. I've got the rennet from the fourth stomach."

"Good gracious!" said Mr Zola, shoving the pot he was holding in his pocket. "How did you manage to do that? I've just been asking about rennet."

"You can't buy it," said Bert. "You have to earn it. Cool moustache, by the way."

Mr Zola proudly twiddled his new facial hair. "Like it?" he asked.

"Your face looks like it's being swallowed up by a huge, hairy slug," said Bert.

"Do you mind! This is Monty the second."

Attila looked Mr Zola up and down. "Who is this man with a hamster on his face?" he asked.

Mr Zola stepped forward. "Gordon Zola – Royal Cheesemaker extraordinaire," he said with a little flourish. "And this is not a hamster but an intricate hair weave, designed to bring Monty back from the dead."

Attila frowned and looked at the twins. "Is he crazy?" he asked.

"Completely," said Bert. "But he *is* the Royal Cheesemaker. Mr Zola, this is Attila. He's taking us with him to the border of Kazakhstan."

"Really?" said Mr Zola, turning to Attila. "I'm supposed to be going to Kazakhstan myself but I crashed my hot air balloon and now find myself rather stuck. I don't suppose I could tag along? Urgent business for the Queen of England and all that."

Attila nodded slowly. "You and your hamster can travel at the rear of the convoy," he said.

"It's not a hamster, it's a—"

But Attila had already marched off.

That afternoon the twins watched as Attila and his people packed their tents, food, furniture and children on to the assembled yaks and ponies.

There were even some goats and a couple of camels. Mr Zola stood beside them fiddling with his Cheesemaker-Locator.

"So I'm changing your registration back to 'CT' for Curd Twins," he said, irritably. "Not that I need the Cheesemaker-Locator to find you two. I can't seem to get away from you."

"We're doing you a favour!" Bert pointed out. "We managed to get a ride to Kazakhstan. Find your own way if you don't want to come with us."

Mr Zola took no notice and wandered off into the jumble of goats and yaks.

The festival seemed to be coming to an end and they were not the only ones getting ready to leave.

"How long does it take to get to the Kazakhstan border?" asked Bert, as Attila marched up and lifted him on to Genghis's broad back.

"We travel overnight to miss the midday sun," he said. "The adults lead the animals, the children sleep on their backs."

Mr Zola popped up from behind a large yak. "I

hope you don't mean that I have to walk all through the night," he said.

"You are an adult, no?" asked Attila.

"Of course I am."

"Then you walk," said Attila. "You can put your hamster on a yak."

Cam and Bert couldn't help giggling as Attila walked away and began lifting the waiting children up on to the small ponies.

"Will someone please tell that infernal man that I do not have a hamster!" yelled Mr Zola. "Monty is beginning to feel quite upset."

Slowly they began to stream out of the festival. Attila was at the front of the convoy. Members of his tribe waved farewell to those left behind. The twins saw Saran waving from her yak-hair tent.

"Goodbye, dear lady," called Mr Zola. "Thank you for restoring Monty to his former glory."

Soon the Yak Festival was left far behind and the sun began to sink towards a huge mountain in the distance.

"That is the great mountain, Tavan Bogd," explained Attila. "It is where Mongolia meets China to the south and Russia to the north. We will trek across the steppe to Kazakhstan."

"I can't see any steps," said Bert.

"The steppe is the grassland of Mongolia," said Attila. "For three thousand years my people have travelled the width and breadth of the steppe. We search for the best campsites and pasture lands for our animals. Our yaks, camels and ponies are very special to us. Every member of this tribe can ride as well as they can walk or run. That is why I am so impressed with your yak skills. But now it is time for you to rest. You have a long journey ahead of you."

"Not as long as me," huffed Mr Zola. "Monty may have had a makeover but he still gets very irritable when he's had no sleep."

The twins bent over their yaks and rested their heads in the deep, long hair.

"How are we supposed to go to sleep while riding a yak?" asked Bert, yawning loudly. "It's impossible."

"I don't know," said Cam, "but I do feel exhausted. It's not every day you win a Mongolian yak race. Well done, Zogs. Well done, Genghis."

She thought that the huge yak mooed back at her, but when she glanced across, she realized that it was just Bert snoring loudly. She smiled and looked round at the flat plains of grassland enclosed by white-tipped mountains. It was very different from home.

*Home*, thought Cam. She leant forward and snuggled into Zogs, closing her eyes. Even if they did get the salt, Kazakhstan was an awfully long way from Cheddar Gorge.

# The Salt Mines of Kazakhstan
## (Two days to go. . .)

The next day was dark and overcast. Cam looked up at the clouds, which were rapidly covering every speck of blue. She glanced over towards Bert. He was lying on his back looking up into the morning sky with his legs dangling over Genghis's two huge horns.

"When we get home," he said. "I'm swapping my bed for a yak. They're far more comfy."

He sat up and stretched deeply as Attila came striding towards them.

"We have arrived at the Kazakhstan border," he said, gravely. "The deserted mines that you seek are in the distance."

"That's great!" cried Bert. "Thanks, Attila. We got here so quickly, we're bound to catch Primula Mold up."

"Where are the mines?" said Cam, jumping off Zog's back.

But the smiles on the twins' faces soon fell away as they looked at the desolation that lay ahead. There wasn't a blade of grass or a single leaf to brighten up the grey grit that covered the terrain in front of them. The occasional boulder rose menacingly from the dry earth. But the worst thing was the huge tangle of bricks and steel in the distance. A collapsed building sank into the rocky landscape like a drowning concrete monster.

Attila tutted and shook his head. "You do not have to go," he said. "You can stay with us, learn the nomadic way of life – herd our goats, milk our yaks. We will teach you how to make *aaruul* – delicious cheese balls."

Bert could feel the hairs on the back of his neck prick to attention as he looked at the abandoned salt mine. He glanced over at Cam. Her eyes were wide but her chin was sticking out determinedly.

"Thanks," she said, "but we have to get back to our grandpa. And we're not going to go home empty-handed, are we, Bert?"

"Nope," he said, simply.

Attila nodded slowly. "Then take this," he said, handing them a torch. "You will need it. And some cheese balls for your journey."

"Thank you, Attila," said Cam, throwing her arms around him. "We'll come back and visit you all, I promise."

"Of course we will," said Bert, hugging Genghis's broad neck. "I'm going to miss you, my hairy friend."

"But I'm coming too," called Mr Zola, rushing up from the back of the convoy.

"I meant Genghis," sighed Bert.

Genghis and Zogs mooed sorrowfully as Cam, Bert

and Mr Zola waved goodbye to Attila and his people and set off across the border into Kazakhstan. Bert offered round the cheese balls. Mr Zola turned his nose up but accepted a few, then checked his Cheesemaker-Locator.

"It seems you've moved up into second place," he said. "There's only Primula Mold ahead of you now. It's looking increasingly likely that she's going to win this competition and I need to find her immediately. I'm supposed to return home with the first person who gets all the ingredients."

"How are you going to get home now you don't have the Crown Balloon?" asked Cam, wondering how she and Bert were going to do it.

"I was hoping to hitch a ride on Primula Mold's balloon," said Mr Zola.

"You'll be lucky," muttered Bert. "We know Primula Mold and she's really mean. She hates people. There's no way she's going to give you a lift home."

Cam stopped walking as an idea popped into her head. "And she won't let you help her make the moose cheese," she added. "She'll want all the glory herself."

"She'll have no choice," said Mr Zola. "It's by royal command."

"It will be a battle, though," continued Cam. "But if you helped us to get the salt, then we would be the leaders. And if you could arrange for us all to go home together, then you could make the moose cheese with us. We'd be happy, you'd be happy, but most importantly, the Queen would be happy. It's a win-win situation."

Mr Zola stroked his moustache and frowned, deep in thought. "I couldn't *help* you get the salt," he said. "That would be against the rules. But if you got it first, then I suppose I could arrange for transportation home. We certainly don't want to stay around here for longer than is necessary."

They all glanced up at the decaying buildings, which were looming nearer. The twins dropped back behind Mr Zola.

"Good one, Cam," whispered Bert. "I was wondering how we were going to get home."

"Well," said Cam, "we need to get the salt first and I have no idea how we're going to manage that."

It was a long walk to the collapsed salt mine. It looked even scarier close up. Rusty railway girders poked out from the crumpled ground. Mounds of rubble and glass were swallowed up by great holes that littered the ruin. The twins peered down a decaying lift shaft. Bert dropped a rock in it. There was a few seconds' silence before they heard it crash into the bottom.

"I reckon that's about a thirty-metre drop," he said.

Mr Zola looked down the shaft just as "God Save the Queen" struck up in his top pocket, reverberating down the mine.

"Your Majesty," he gushed. "Nearly there now, ma'am, just one ingredient to go. . . I do realize that time is running out. . . I understand we must leave enough time to make and mature the cheese before Monsieur Grand-Fromage arrives. . . I will hurry the contestants along. . . At once,

168

ma'am . . . as soon as possible. . . . You can rely on me, ma'am."

He replaced the red phone. "The Queen is getting jittery," he said. "She's worried nobody will be back in time to make the cheese. It needs to be matured overnight before serving. Monsieur Grand-Fromage is arriving the day after tomorrow and—"

CLANK  CLANK  CLANK

He stopped mid-sentence as a banging sound floated up from the old mine shaft. It was getting louder and coming closer.

CLANK  CLANK  CLANK

It was followed by a low howl.

"What is that?" cried Mr Zola, hiding behind Cam.

The twins slowly backed off as the hammering and howling came nearer.

"It's the evil spirits," whispered Bert. "They're coming for us. They're annoyed that I threw a rock down the mine."

"I can smell them!" gasped Mr Zola.

A vile vapour wafted up from the hole in the ground. The hammering stopped. Cam held her breath and instinctively pulled Bert back as a spindly figure slowly emerged from the shaft. The hunched creature hauled itself out of the hole and turned towards them. Two bulging black eyes stared out from beneath a bright light glowing from a wrinkled white forehead.

"IT *IS* AN EVIL SPIRIT!" screamed Mr Zola, running away. "IT WASN'T ME THAT THREW THE ROCK. IT WAS THE BOY! TAKE THE BOY!"

Mr Zola disappeared into the distance. The twins looked back at the old woman in front of them, her lucky Stilton swinging from her neck and a whining basset hound in a basket on her back. Bert felt the familiar wave of uneasiness trickle through his body whenever Primula Mold was near. But he stepped forward and focused, as he always did, on her dog instead.

"Hello," he said, vaguely. "Hey, Fungus. What's the matter? Did you not like it down there?"

Fungus jumped out of the basket and ran towards Bert, his tail wagging happily. Primula Mold put down her climbing hammer, turned off her head torch and removed the spiked shoes that had helped her to scale the old lift shaft.

"He's howling because he was nearly hit by a rock," she snapped. "Who threw it?"

Bert turned scarlet. "Sorry," he muttered. "I didn't know anyone was down there."

"Hmph! Thoughtless behaviour! But I would expect nothing more from you. Anyway, I see you finally decided to take part in the Great Moose Cheese Chase. So where is he, then? Where's your grandfather?"

It was Cam's turn to go red. "We came on our own," she murmured.

Miss Mold looked shocked. "I'm surprised he allowed that," she croaked. "You two are up to no good again. I can see it in your eyes. But if you think you're going to win, then you're mistaken."

She held up a gleaming rock-salt crystal. "I've

got all the ingredients now and I'm heading home. Come along, Fungus."

The dog gave Bert a lick and trotted over to his mistress.

"I will expect a curtsey from you next time we meet. And you may address me as 'Lady Mold'."

She stalked towards a collapsed building. The twins spotted her yellow balloon anchored beside it.

"And after I win I'm going to look into buying your land with the prize money," she said.

Bert stomped after her, all nerves forgotten. "You can't do that!" he cried. "Gramps will never sell it to you."

"We shall see," called Miss Mold, climbing into the basket and heaving Fungus in beside her. "The Queen is bound to grant me some favours when I produce my *special* moose cheese."

Mr Zola appeared from behind a large rock just as Primula Mold released the ropes and sailed off into the grey sky.

"Did someone mention moose cheese?" he called.

"That was Primula Mold," said Bert, pointing towards the balloon. "You missed her. You're too late."

"Let's just hope we're not," whispered Cam.

# 18

## Cataclysm

Mr Zola came running over.

"I should have known that was Primula Mold," he said, checking his Cheesemaker-Locator. "Why didn't you tell me she looked like an evil mine monster?"

He began to sprint after the yellow hot air balloon. "Miss Mold," he shouted. "Miss Mold, take me with you. I'm the Royal Cheesemaker. I'm commanded by the Queen to oversee this competition. I must accompany the winner home and help them make the moose cheese to Her Majesty's exact taste."

"I don't need any help to make cheese from a young whippersnapper like you," called Miss Mold as she floated away. "I'm going to delight Her Majesty with a surprise ingredient."

Mr Zola watched as Primula Mold's balloon became a tiny speck in the sky.

"Her Majesty doesn't like surprises," he muttered, sinking to the ground, "and I'm supposed to keep up with the leader. She's going to be furious."

"We could still be the leaders," urged Cam. "If you could just think of a faster way to get us home, Mr Zola, then Bert and I will somehow get the salt."

Mr Zola sat for a moment in deep thought. Then he jumped to his feet.

"You're right," he cried, reaching for his phone. "I need to call in an old favour."

"Are you calling the Queen?"

"No, she's still fuming about the Crown Balloon. I need to find a different way to get us back without concerning the Queen. You two look for a way into the mine. Quick as you can; we must hurry."

The twins left Mr Zola talking into his phone. Bert

picked up Miss Mold's discarded hammer and they started to explore the crumpled buildings. There were several gaping holes which dropped into the darkness, but the surrounding rock was too crumbly to climb down without the right equipment.

"I wish Miss Mold had left her spiked climbing shoes behind as well," said Bert. "We have to find a safe way in as quickly as possible."

They ran along the old railway track. The rail was bent and buckled in places but smoothed out and sloped down steeply into a pile of rubble stacked against a rock face.

"The miners must have used this track to transport the salt," said Cam. "I bet it leads underground. Help me move this rubble, Bert. I think there might be a tunnel behind it."

It was hard work moving the large stones off the track and away from the rock face, but Cam was right. Behind them was a small tunnel sloping down into the ground beyond. Sitting on the track inside the hidden tunnel was a cart. It looked like there was a small see-saw on top.

"Why would they have a see-saw on top of a railway cart?" asked Bert, climbing on board. "C'mon, Cam, get on the other side."

The moment Cam sat on the opposite end of the see-saw the little cart began to move along the track.

"It's not a see-saw," she gasped. "It's a pumping cart. The more we go up and down, the faster it gets."

"Well, what are we waiting for?" said Bert. "Let's go."

"Wait, where's the torch that Attila gave us?"

But Bert wasn't listening and began jumping up and down on his half of the see-saw. The cart started picking up speed, then plummeted down a sharp dip, plunging them into total darkness and shooting along the track.

"BERT!" screamed Cam. "What have you done?"

The twins flew down the railway, no longer in control of the cart. The see-saw on top was throwing them up and down. Their stomachs were left far behind as sharp bends followed steep dips, flinging them from side to side. Suddenly, the cart struck something on the track and came to an abrupt halt, throwing them clear off the truck and on to the hard ground.

Cam lay there for a moment before staggering to her feet. A large bump was slowly growing on the back of her head. She reached up and touched it carefully with one hand, steadying herself against the wall with the other. It was pitch black and she couldn't see a thing. She felt the cold, hard rock beneath her fingers. Something brushed against the back of her hand and she pulled it away sharply.

"B-Bert?"

Her anxious voice bounced off the damp walls and fell into thick silence. She began fumbling in her coat for the torch but her fingers were numb. She took a deep breath, trying to quell the rising panic.

"Bert? Where are you? Are you all right?"

Something scuttled past her on the wall, hissing softly. She backed away, still feeling for the torch, and tripped over a large lump on the floor.

"OW!" yelled Bert. "Watch where you're going!"

"Oh, thank goodness that's you," cried Cam, reaching for her brother. "Are you hurt?"

"No, not much," he said, rubbing his temple and slowly getting to his feet. "My head aches, though."

"Mine too," she whispered. "But that's the least of our problems. I don't think we're alone. Listen, there's something else down here."

They stood huddled together. The low hissing sound seemed to be coming from all around them.

"Where's the torch?" gulped Bert.

Cam finally managed to pull it out of her coat with a shaking hand and pressed the switch. The moment it lit up the hissing stopped. It took a moment for the twins' eyes to get used to the light. They were in a low rocky chamber. Rotten wooden pillars held up the crumbling ceiling and the grey stone walls were covered in large brown patches.

Bert took a deep breath. "I'm not scared of heights," he said. "I'm not scared of wild animals or going fast or anything like that. But I don't like enclosed spaces that smell like death."

It was hard to breathe properly. The air was thick with a heavy stench. Far worse than the large piles of manure they had on the farm.

"Do you really think this place is haunted?" asked Bert. "Or was that hissing noise inside our heads?"

"Let's just find the salt and get out of here," said Cam. "We'll have to see-saw back the way we came. Unfortunately, it's all uphill."

"OK. Keep looking as we go. Primula Mold's salt was like a crystal. It must be embedded in the stone."

They looked up at the rocks surrounding them.

"The walls almost look like they're moving in the light," whispered Cam, taking a step closer. As she walked, something crunched beneath her feet. She pointed the torch down and shrieked as something ran over her foot.

"The walls *are* moving!" cried Bert. "Hold up the torch!"

As the light hit the wall the brown patches that speckled the grey rocks hissed and scuttled up on to the ceiling. Cam screamed again and jumped backwards.

"Cockroaches!" warned Bert. "Hundreds of them. Look, they're covering everything."

Swarms of cockroaches skittered over the walls and along the floor.

"Get back in the cart!" screeched Cam, swiping one off Bert's shoulder. "Move!"

She clambered back into the truck and held the light up for Bert.

"Wait," he said. "I think I saw something glinting over there."

"Just get in!" yelled Cam.

"Hold the lamp up again."

Reluctantly Cam did as she was asked. The torch revealed a smaller tunnel leading off the main chamber with a tiny sparkle of light at the end.

"We've got to check that out," said Bert.

Cam shook her head vigorously.

"Do you want to win this competition or not? Cockroaches can't hurt you. They just smell and hiss and . . . maybe have a little nibble, but . . . forget that bit."

Cam gritted her teeth and climbed back out of

the cart, trying to ignore the crunch as her feet landed on the floor.

"They hate light," said Bert. "Just hold it up and they'll scuttle away."

They edged their way along the narrow tunnel, Bert in front and Cam close behind. She kept feeling the odd cockroach scramble up her leg or run across her back, and swiped them off wildly.

"It's all right," said Bert. "Try to keep calm. Let's sing to take our mind off them."

He began to sing to the tune of, "I Do Like To Be Beside the Seaside".

"Oh, I do like to be inside a mine-shaft! Where the cockroaches smell like rotting flesh—"

"OK, that's not helping," interrupted Cam. "Look! I think I can see something glinting up ahead."

Just in front of them, poking out of the wall, was a small crystal of rock salt.

"Wow! I told you," cried Bert. "I can't believe we've found some. But it doesn't look a lot. How much do we need?"

"I suppose that depends on how salty the Queen likes her moose cheese. Let's just get it and go."

Bert pulled out the climbing hammer and began to bash the wall. The whole tunnel started to shake. Bits of earth tumbled from the ceiling.

"Careful!" cried Cam.

"Nearly there," he said, smashing away at the wall.

The salt crystal fell into his hands just as a loud rumble filled the whole mine. Cam held the torch up and looked along the tunnel towards the noise. A large cloud of dust was flying through the air towards them.

"It's collapsing!" she screamed. "The whole thing is coming down!"

"Go!" cried Bert, pushing Cam forward.

They raced back the way they came, to where the old pumping cart stood, and then jumped aboard it. Swarms of cockroaches scattered as the cloud of dust and rock exploded into the chamber.

"See-saw like you've never see-sawed before!" yelled Bert.

The twins furiously jumped up and down on either side of the pump, propelling the cart along the track. They shot into a rising tunnel just as the chamber behind them completely collapsed.

"FASTER!" screamed Cam, looking over Bert's shoulder.

A rumbling smog of crashing rocks chased them up the tunnel. The twins bounced up and down as fast as they could but it was all uphill and soon they were engulfed in a veil of rock dust and earth.

"Keep pumping," coughed Bert. "I can see a circle of light up ahead."

Cam could no longer see Bert even though he was just centimetres in front of her. She was facing the collapsing mine and her lungs began to fill with dirt. Her legs turned to jelly with the lack of oxygen and she slumped to the floor of the cart. A large rock smashed into the ground beside her, quickly followed by several more. The avalanche was upon them and she closed her eyes, waiting to be completely flattened, when suddenly they emerged into daylight. She looked up to see Bert pumping the cart along with his hands. He was completely covered in dust but didn't stop until they were clear of the tunnel.

"Cam, can you move?" he shouted, pulling her from the cart. "The whole place is falling deeper into the ground. We've got to get out of here."

Cam lurched to her feet. The earth beneath them was shaking and large cracks were shooting along the ground.

"RUN!" yelled Bert.

But a huge crevice appeared ahead of them, swallowing up their only route to escape.

# 19

## The Whisker Club

The wide crack opened up in front of the twins, deafening them with the sound of imploding rocks. There was nowhere to go. They desperately looked from left to right when a loud thumping noise came from high above them. They looked up to see Mr Zola dangling from a rope attached to a large military helicopter. He swung in and caught hold of Bert, who grabbed Cam just as the ground beneath them disappeared into a black hole. The twins clung to each other, the wind twirling them around as they were slowly winched aboard.

They sat panting on the helicopter floor. Cam began coughing and couldn't stop. A young man dressed in an RAF uniform patted her on the back and wrapped them both up in a silver blanket. He handed them mugs of steaming tea.

"You'll be OK," he said to Cam. "You've just breathed in a bit of dust. Drink plenty and don't worry about coughing. It's just your body getting rid of all that dirt."

"Thank you, Flight Lieutenant," said Mr Zola, accepting a mug from him.

The young man nodded and took a seat next to the pilot at the front of the helicopter. Mr Zola inspected the twins over his tea.

"That was a close shave," he said. "How was it down there?"

"It was horrible," spluttered Cam. "Full of cockroaches."

Mr Zola pulled a face and covered his moustache with both hands.

"Thank goodness Monty wasn't there," he said in a loud whisper. "He has a thing about bugs, especially . . . hair lice."

"Cockroaches are about a hundred times bigger than lice," said Bert, "and a lot smellier."

"Too much information," gasped Mr Zola. "Let's move on. Did you get the salt?"

"The salt?" repeated Cam. "Yes, but more importantly we got away with our lives . . . thanks to Bert."

She smiled at her brother. "Good job," she said. "Maybe you're not such a yak brain."

"Don't thank him, thank me," said Mr Zola. "I'm the one who got you out of there. Our pilot today is Captain Mouthbrow-Smythe, an old friend from my RAF Whisker Club days. All members swear an oath to help fellow comrades in need. He and his fine nose fringe will be flying us back to Cheddar Gorge."

The pilot turned around and smiled at the twins, his thick black moustache twitching proudly.

They grinned back.

"We're going home," coughed Cam. "Back to Cheddar Gorge, back to Whey Farm, back to. . ."

She stopped coughing and looked anxiously at Bert.

". . .Gramps," he finished. "He's going to be furious."

Mr Zola looked from one twin to the other. "Why will he be furious? You said your grandfather sent you on this mission. I ticked the parental consent box and you gave me a letter."

Cam turned bright red. She hoped Mr Zola didn't notice under all the dust she was still caked in.

"When I said he sent us," she muttered, "what I meant was . . . he *didn't* send us. I wrote that note."

Mr Zola's white skin grew visibly paler beneath the black swirls of Monty. "But if your grandfather hasn't given his consent, then you'll be disqualified. We won't be able to make the moose cheese and I'll be in trouble with the Queen. You have deceived me!"

Bert bit his lip. "Once Gramps sees that we've got all the ingredients," he said, "I'm sure he'll give his consent."

"Especially if the Royal Cheesemaker asks him," added Cam. "He's a sucker for anything royal."

Mr Zola seemed to calm down slightly. Bert

thought he could actually see his brain ticking over.

"I can be very persuasive when I want to be," Mr Zola said, eventually. "OK, I will sort out this mess when we arrive in Cheddar Gorge. I assume there's a dairy at your farm?"

"Yes, of course," replied Cam.

"We're running out of time," said Mr Zola. "The State Banquet is the day after tomorrow. So, if we can make the moose cheese on your farm when we get back, then let it mature overnight in the caves at Cheddar Gorge, it will be ready just in time. Let's hope your grandfather forgives you when he sees you're going to win the competition."

"That's if Primula Mold doesn't get there first," said Bert.

Mr Zola checked his Cheesemaker-Locator. "This helicopter flies at two hundred and seventy-five miles per hour," he said. "We should be passing her in precisely twenty-three minutes."

Cam threw off her blanket and began dancing around the helicopter, completely forgetting about her cough.

"I can't believe we've done it," she said. "We've beaten everyone. We're going to win."

"Lord Curd," sighed Bert. "I think I should present the moose cheese to the Queen. After all, I got two out of the three ingredients."

Cam stopped dancing. "So?" she snapped. "I won the rennet, which was the hardest ingredient to get."

"What? Harder than getting salt from a collapsing mine?" cried Bert. "Which I had to rescue you from!"

"The only reason you had to rescue me was because *you* made the whole thing come crashing down. And besides, *I* saved you when you nearly fell off the Trans-Siberian train."

Mr Zola sighed and unravelled the curling stems of his new bushy moustache. They were very long when they were straightened out and he managed to stuff both ends into his ears.

"I saved you, no *I* saved *you*," he mimicked. "I was hoping that working together would put a stop to all this bickering. Actually, Monty and I saved both of you from being swallowed up by the ground and sometimes we wonder why. Don't we, Monty?"

"I suppose that's because we just happen to have some Siberian moose milk, Mongolian rennet and Kazakh salt!" said Cam.

"Sorry, can't hear you properly," muttered Mr Zola, reaching for a flask and pouring out three bowls of hot tomato soup. "No more arguing. Eat up your soup. By the time we've had some supper and a decent night's sleep, we'll be home."

The twins forgot their argument and tucked in. They hadn't eaten since that morning and they were very hungry. As the helicopter flew across Western Asia and on over Europe, Bert imagined what it would be like to be Lord Curd. First of all, he would ban Primula Mold from coming anywhere near their farm. Fungus could visit, though. Then he might build an animal sanctuary. They could have all sorts of animals – cows, goats, cats, dogs. Gramps would like that.

Cam was thinking about winning too. She would expand the farm. Maybe bring some yaks over from

Mongolia. Attila could help them. Yak cheese was delicious. It was bound to sell well. Gramps would be so proud.

They were going to win. Nothing could go wrong now.

# 20

# Making a Moose Cheese
## (One day to go...)

Bert rubbed his eyes. He was still dusty from the previous day. He sat listening to the buzz of the helicopter blades. Mr Zola was talking into his red phone.

"Yes, ma'am... the two children from Cheddar Gorge... they are the new leaders... The moose cheese should be ready in plenty of time. It only needs twelve hours to mature... I will, ma'am... Thank you, ma'am..."

Bert peered out of the window. A valley of

green spread out beneath them.

"Cam!" he cried. "Look, we're home. We're home!"

Cam opened her eyes and sat up, yawning loudly. "Are we here already?" she mumbled as the flight lieutenant came into the cabin.

"Captain Mouthbrow-Smythe would like to inform you that we will be landing in Cheddar Gorge in approximately three minutes," he said.

"Thank you, Flight Lieutenant," said Mr Zola.

Cam jumped up and looked out. "I can see the gorge!"

Cheddar Gorge looked even more impressive from the air. The enormous cleft split the green hills into two jagged halves. The limestone cliffs were surrounded on three sides by a glorious lush quilt of rolling fields and woodland with the village of Cheddar snuggled into the west side.

"There's the reservoir," cried Bert, pointing to a completely round lake glinting like a huge penny. "And there's our farm, right on top of the gorge. I can see the cows. Hello, cows! I've missed you!"

The cattle moved hurriedly away as the helicopter came in to land on a field beside Whey Farm. It began to rain. Mr Zola and the twins jumped out, covering their ears as the wind from the revolving blades whisked up the raindrops. Cam and Bert waved to Captain Mouthbrow-Smythe and the flight lieutenant, who were sitting in the cockpit. The flight lieutenant saluted and Captain Mouthbrow-Smythe twiddled his fine moustache as the great machine rose back up into the sky. Mr Zola stood to attention and twiddled back. When the helicopter was out of sight, they began to make their way over to the farmhouse.

"I'm really looking forward to seeing Gramps again," said Cam. "But I'm dreading it too."

"I think I had better talk to him first," said Mr Zola. "You take the ingredients over to the dairy while I explain to your grandfather what has happened and get his permission. I'll smooth everything over. I might be some time, though, so you had better get started. Break up the rock salt. It must be ground into a fine powder. But don't do anything else. I shall heat the milk and add the rennet when I return. It's a delicate procedure and if you do it wrong then the whole cheese will be ruined. Do I make myself clear?"

They both nodded. Mr Zola strode off through the rain in the direction of the farmhouse. The twins ran over to the large outbuilding that was their dairy.

"I hope Gramps isn't too mad," said Cam, pulling open the huge door.

"I know," sighed Bert. "I can almost hear his pocket change jingling from here."

The dairy had been converted from an old barn and still had the high vaulted ceiling and big wooden beams. They walked through the cattle stalls. Each one had a trough full of hay at the front and a milking stool and bucket behind. Gramps still preferred to milk the cows by hand and refused to invest in the latest milking machines. A large kitchen lay through a door at the far end. A wooden table took up most of the room, with a green range cooker filling the back wall. Various cheeses hung from the beams, tied up tightly in white muslin.

"Ah, it's good to be home," said Bert, sniffing the air. "Right, let's get going."

He took the rock crystal out of his pocket and handed it to Cam. It was still muddy and dusty. She held it under the tap at the deep sink. As the dirt slid away, a shaft of light pierced through the window and bounced off the gleaming crystal, lighting up the whole room.

"Wow!" she cried. "It's beautiful! It's like a diamond. No wonder it's so valuable."

"Yeah," sniffed Bert, squinting against the brightness. "Bash it up, then."

Cam sighed and dried the salt crystal.

"It seems such a shame," she said, placing it gently on the table. "I can see a rainbow inside it."

"Yeah, rainbow," said Bert, bringing a huge rolling pin smashing down on top of it.

CRASH!

Fragments of salt flew across the table as the crystal splintered into hundreds of pieces.

"Bert!" cried Cam. "You're such a gorilla!"

He gave the remaining piece of salt another big bash.

"We haven't got time for all this *ooh isn't it beautiful* rubbish," he said. "Once we've added the milk and rennet, we have to let the curds separate from the whey and then we've got to mature it overnight. I bet Primula Mold is nearly home. She could still beat us."

Cam marched past him to the range. "You do the salt then," she muttered, getting a steel pan down from the wall. "I'll get everything else ready."

An hour passed. Bert had finished breaking up the salt and was scraping every last grain off the table into a bowl. Cam anxiously fiddled with a large wooden spoon.

"Where are they?" she said.

"I bet Gramps is still furious," replied Bert. "He's

going to take a lot of persuading. I'll go and see what's going on."

But just as he reached the door, Mr Zola came bursting through. He was very wet and his jacket was torn. Monty was a tangled mess and drooped sadly down his chin.

"What's happened?" cried Bert. "Where's Gramps?"

"Don't worry, everything is fine," panted Mr Zola. "We finally have your grandfather's consent, so can continue making the moose cheese."

"Where is he?" asked Cam. "Was he angry?"

"Yes he was," said Mr Zola. "But when he found out that you were en route to winning the competition he soon changed his mind. He even took me down to the caves of Cheddar Gorge to show me a good place to mature the moose cheese overnight. That's why I'm in such a state. All this rain has made everything very wet and I slipped whilst trying to climb back up, ripped my clothes and terrified poor Monty. Your grandfather is still down there arranging some of his own cave-aged cheddars. He said to meet him there when the moose cheese is finished. How's the salt looking?"

He walked over to the table and ran his fingers through the ground salt.

"Doesn't Gramps want to come and help make it?" asked Bert, his face falling.

"No," replied Mr Zola. "He said he would leave it to me because I know how Her Majesty likes it. Now let's get going. We haven't got much time. That salt is perfect, well done. We'll need seven cups of milk to make a good-sized cheese. Have we got that much?"

"Just," said Cam, measuring it out into the steel pan.

"Next, heat the moose milk very gradually to sixty-five degrees Fahrenheit. It must be precise. The production of moose cheese is an exact science. Any hotter, any colder, and it will be ruined. Do you understand?"

"Of course I do," said Cam, stirring it gently with the wooden spoon. "I know how to make cheese. I was Junior Cheddar Champion, remember?"

"Runner-up!" corrected Bert, grabbing a thermometer.

"Moose cheese has to be perfect," said Mr Zola. "There's no room for mistakes."

Cam continued stirring while Bert checked the temperature.

"OK," he said after a couple of minutes, "we're up to temp in five, four, three, two, one!"

"Right, add the salt," barked Mr Zola. "Three level teaspoons. Make sure they're level! Keep stirring! Not too fast! Not too slow! Don't stop!"

Cam glanced up at Mr Zola as she stirred the milk. His face was flushed and Monty was fluttering so rapidly, there was a slight breeze.

"Now, for the rennet," cried Mr Zola. "I'll do this bit."

A bead of sweat trickled from his forehead and fell on to the stove, narrowly missing the moose-cheese mix.

"If you two could just leave me alone for a moment," he said, grabbing the wooden spoon from Cam. "I need to concentrate."

"But you haven't got any rennet," said Cam. "I have."

Mr Zola stopped stirring for a moment and stared at her.

"Yes . . . yes, of course you have," he said. "Well, hand it over."

Cam reached into her inside pocket and gave him the small ceramic pot.

"Off you go, then," he said, slipping it into his own pocket.

The twins hesitated at the door.

"But I want to help you add the rennet," said Bert.

"It's just a brown liquid," replied Mr Zola. "Nothing that you haven't seen before. Go on, you're putting me off already. Remember, this cheese has to be made to the Queen's exact taste and she's very fussy about her rennet. I'll call you when I'm done."

Cam and Bert wandered out of the kitchen, shutting the door behind them.

"Strange," said Cam. "He couldn't get rid of us quick enough."

She grabbed hold of Bert's arm, making him jump in the air.

"Bert!" she cried. "What if he's planning to steal our cheese?"

# 21

## The Cave

Bert clenched his fists and turned back towards the kitchen. "He'd better not," he fumed.

"Wait," said Cam. "Let's spy on him through the keyhole."

The twins jostled for position outside the door.

"He'll hear us," she whispered. "I'll tell you what's happening."

She bent down and put her eye to the hole in the lock. Mr Zola was fumbling around in his jacket pocket. He had his back to them so Cam couldn't see his face. Eventually he pulled out two pots, stared at them and returned one to his pocket.

"What's he doing?"

"He's getting the rennet out of his pocket," said Cam. "Now he's adding one, two, three teaspoons. He's stirring the pan—"

Bert nudged Cam out of the way. "Let me see," he said, bending his head to the keyhole. "He's turned around. He's laughing. He's walking towards us – quick!"

The twins jumped away from the door just as it was flung open.

"All done!" said Mr Zola, a huge smile still spread across his face. "Now all we have to do is let it cool, separate the curds from the whey, press the curd into a round mould and leave to settle in a cold dark place. . . Is everything all right?"

The twins looked guiltily up at him.

"We thought you were going to steal our cheese," admitted Bert.

Mr Zola looked hurt. "My dear boy," he said. "After everything we've been through together?"

"Sorry," mumbled Cam. "You just seemed a

bit . . . you know . . . weird."

"That's because I am *a-bit-you-know-weird*," said Mr Zola. "I always get excited when I'm making cheese. Come along; let's get cleaned up and have something to eat while we're waiting for it to cool. It's fine with your grandfather."

They made their way back to the farmhouse and all had a wash. The twins changed their dirty clothes before finding some bread and jam in the kitchen. When they returned to the dairy, thick clumps of cheese curd had formed in the pot on the range. Mr Zola ladled them out and pushed them into a round mould.

"Have a sniff," he said. "The sweet smell of moose cheese. The rarest cheese in the world. You may never get to see one again. Savour the moment."

The moose cheese looked amazing. It was a thick creamy yellow but speckled with tiny fragments of crystal that sparkled in the light, creating a warm glow all around it.

"It looks like a UFO," shouted Bert, excitedly.

"It's beautiful," said Cam. "Can we taste a bit?"

"No!" cried Mr Zola. "This is for the Queen, and the Queen alone."

"And Mr Grand-Fromage," added Bert.

"Yes, him too," murmured Mr Zola. "Now, back to the cheddar caves to meet your grandfather. The moose cheese can mature overnight and be ready for the State Banquet tomorrow, where you two will receive your titles."

It had taken all day to make the cheese and it was starting to get dark. The rain still fell heavily. The twins ran ahead of Mr Zola who covered the moose cheese with his coat. They scrambled down a steep path that led to the cheddar caves embedded in the gorge. Mr Zola pointed to a wide crack in the rock face.

"Here we are," he said. "I took the liberty of bringing a torch from the farmhouse."

The twins stopped short of the cave entrance.

"That's not the right one," said Cam. "Gramps won't be in there. We know these cliffs and caves. Gramps says never to go in that one. It's connected to an underground river and can flood."

"I'm sure it was this one," said Mr Zola. "Let me just check."

He stepped into the shallow cave. "You're right, it's not the one your grandfather showed me," he called. "But it's much better. It's perfect! Exactly the right temperature and humidity for moose cheese – and look! We don't have to go far in. There's a high shelf just inside the opening."

The twins followed him inside and watched as he placed the moose cheese on a flat shelf of rock that jutted out high up on the wall.

"It should be safe up there," he said. "It's only for a few hours."

"But Gramps said never to go in this cave," insisted Bert.

Mr Zola sighed and turned to face him. "I am the expert on where moose cheese should be matured, young man," he said. "However, if it would make you feel better, we can investigate this underground river just in case. When we meet up with your grandfather we will double-check with him, OK?"

He flashed the torch to the back of the cave. It was much longer than it first appeared. A narrow tunnel led deeper into the earth. Mr Zola made his way over and peered into it.

"Whispering whiskers! There's an opening at the end of this tunnel," he said. "And look, I can just make out some stalactites hanging from the ceiling."

The twins followed him into the tunnel. They were curious, as it was one of the only caves that they hadn't explored. They came out into an immense cavern. Mr Zola shone the torch along a huge tiered wall which was completely covered by a great cascade of multicoloured stalactites. Around the perimeter several colossal stalagmite pillars rose from the floor.

"It's like a cathedral," whispered Cam.

At the far end of the cavern a shallow pool reflected the jagged ceiling above.

"See, there *is* water in here," said Bert. "I think we should find another cave." He turned to go but stopped in his tracks as a faint cry echoed through the cavern.

"What was that?" he whispered.

They all stopped.

"Help!"

"There it is again," cried Cam. "Someone's down here. HELLO?"

Her voice rebounded off the walls.

"Help!"

"It's coming from over here," said Mr Zola, heading deeper into the cavern. "Stay close to me; we don't want to get lost. Here, catch hold of this." He threw a length of rope to Bert.

"It's from the helicopter," he explained. "If I tie it round your wrist and then around Cam's we won't get separated. I'll hang on to the other end."

They wound their way around the stalagmites protruding from the ground. The cavern narrowed the further along they went.

"Help!"

"It's getting louder," said Bert. "HOLD ON. WE'RE COMING."

They eventually reached a narrow alley.

"You go first, Bert," said Mr Zola. "I'll shine the

light from behind so that we can all see where we're going."

They squeezed into the thin passage and edged their way along. Mr Zola's torch lit up a small grotto at the end.

"Over here," called a familiar voice from the chamber.

"Gramps!" yelled the twins together.

They burst into the grotto to see Gramps tied to a rocky stalagmite.

"Cam, Bert!" he shouted, his face lighting up. But it clouded over as Mr Zola followed them in.

"No!" Gramps growled. "Not you!"

# 22

## Revenge
### (Twelve hours to go. . .)

The twins turned to Mr Zola. His eyes were glowing and Monty was standing on end like a startled cat. He caught hold of the other end of the rope that was tying Cam and Bert together and quick as a flash looped it over a tall thin stalagmite.

"Mr Zola!" screamed Cam as he jerked them against the rock. "What are you doing?"

But he had already pulled the rope tight, securing the twins to the stalagmite. He looped the rope around their bodies, squeezing their backs against the hard rock.

"Let us go!" yelled Bert, struggling furiously against the rope.

"Leave them alone!" bellowed Gramps.

"I'm sorry, old chap," panted Mr Zola. He was sweating from the exertion of binding the twins. "But I want revenge!.."

"What for?" cried Bert. "We've done nothing wrong."

"Not you, dear boy," said Mr Zola. "It's nothing personal, you understand."

He stood by the narrow exit and twiddled Monty back into place.

"It's the Queen," he announced.

The twins' eyebrows simultaneously pinged to the top of their heads.

"If you touch one quaffed hair on the royal head," roared Gramps, "then I'll . . . I'll—"

"Your threats won't dissuade me," interrupted Mr Zola. "I am going to avenge the death of my father. He died by moose and so shall she. My father was killed whilst trying to milk a moose to make cheese for the Queen. If it wasn't for her then he would still be here. I've been waiting, biding my time, ingratiating myself into the royal circle, ready to take my revenge. When she announced this competition I knew it was my chance. All I had to do was stick with the leaders and make sure I was present when the cheese was prepared. While you two were racing those yaks, trying to win the rennet from the fourth stomach, I was obtaining the rennet from the third stomach."

"The poisonous one!" cried the twins together.

"Deadly!" said Mr Zola, holding up a red pot with a black skull and crossbones on the label. "Protocol demands that the Queen has the first mouthful of moose cheese. She will then have approximately two point four seconds to live."

Mr Zola turned to go.

"I knew you were up to something," cried Gramps. "The moment you walked into the farmhouse and tried to persuade me to let the children make the moose cheese. That's why I wouldn't give my consent."

"You told us Gramps agreed," gasped Bert.

Mr Zola rolled his eyes. "I lied," he said. "Your grandfather was still furious with you for entering the competition. He refused to allow you to take part. That would have ruined my plan and time was running out."

"I could sense you and your trumped-up moustache were up to no good," shouted Gramps.

Mr Zola looked furious. "Leave Monty out of this," he snarled. "If you had given your permission then we wouldn't be here now."

"If I'd said yes then we would have been blamed for the poisoned moose cheese," spluttered Gramps.

"Yes, it would have been perfect," muttered Mr Zola. "But you had to say no. So I have to hide you away down here until the job is done. I shall tell the Queen that you have temporarily gone missing. She won't have time to question me, as Monsieur Grand-Fromage will have arrived by then."

"You can't keep us here!" cried Cam.

"I'll leave a torch," said Mr Zola. "My argument is not with you, although you can be very annoying.

I shall pass on a note to the authorities detailing your whereabouts. But by that time it will be too late to save the Queen, and Monty and I will have escaped to Acapulco. Mexico is one of the top three moustache-dense countries of the world. We will blend in, never to be seen again."

Monty fluttered manically as Mr Zola laughed. "Farewell, dear cheese-urchins," he said, disappearing into the narrow passage. "I don't think I could have done it without you."

Cam looked over at Gramps, who was tied to the stalagmite next to theirs. She could just see his anxious face lit up by the torch left on a nearby boulder.

"We're sorry, Gramps," she said. "This is all our fault."

"Yes," muttered Bert. "Sorry."

"At least you're safe," sighed Gramps, "which is more than can be said for the Queen. How long have we got before the State Banquet on top of the gorge?"

"It starts tomorrow morning," replied Cam.

"That gives us a bit of time," said Gramps, pulling at the ropes that bound him. "Let's get out of here."

They spent the next few hours wriggling their wrists, trying unsuccessfully to loosen the knots.

"It's impossible," said Bert at last. "It's really tight."

They all drooped against their ropes, exhausted from struggling.

"I'm hungry," said Bert.

"And I'm thirsty," added Cam. "So thirsty that I think I can actually hear running water."

"Me too," murmured Gramps.

"Me three," whispered Bert.

They all looked up towards the sound of trickling water. A round hole in the side of the cave was leaking a steady stream of crystal-clear liquid on to the cave floor.

"Heaven help us," cried Gramps. "It's the underground river. All this rain has caused it to break its banks. We're going to be flooded!"

# 23

## The Flood

### (Six hours to go. . .)

The water from the underground river poured steadily out of the hole and down the wall. A small pool began to form directly underneath it. Gramps and the twins watched as a little trickle broke away from the main puddle and snaked towards them, circling their feet.

"Looks like we haven't got much time," said Gramps, trying to keep his voice calm. The twins looked at him, fear darkening their faces.

"I don't want to die in a cold, dark place," said

Bert. "In fact, I don't want to die in a warm, light place either."

"What are we going to do?" cried Cam.

Gramps glanced down at the water, which was now covering the floor. "I'll tell you exactly what we're going to do," he said. "You two need to pull alternately against the rope that's binding you together. If you rub it against the stalagmite, eventually, the rope will fray and break. I'll do what I can but I can't seem to move at all. Once you're free, you can untie me."

The twins nodded and began tugging at their rope.

"Not like that," said Cam. "If we pull at the same time then we'll never get anywhere."

"You're doing it wrong," replied Bert.

"You are!"

"Pull when I say."

"No, you pull when I say."

"Stop fighting!" yelled Gramps. "For the love of cheese, why can't you work together?"

Cam and Bert looked down at their feet. Their shoes were now completely covered in water.

"We can," said Bert. "We had to during the Great Moose Cheese Chase."

"And what happened?" asked Gramps.

"We nearly won."

"Exactly!" cried Gramps. "Now get a move on!"

The twins began pulling the rope alternately. It didn't move very much because they were so tightly bound, but even the smallest of movements helped.

"That's it," said Gramps. "You're doing it. Keep going."

They couldn't see each other's faces, as they both had their backs against the stalagmite. But as they settled into a rhythm it was almost as if they could sense what the other was doing. It was slow, exhausting work and they had to stop several times to catch their breath. All the time, little by little, the freezing water was rising. It lapped around their legs, turning them to ice and making everything harder. The sound of the constant stream pouring from the hole was hard to ignore.

"Try not to think about the water," called

221

Gramps. "You're doing really well. I can see a nick in the rope."

Cam's teeth started chattering. "M-my wrists are raw," she stuttered. "We've been trying for hours and I'm so c-cold. I don't know if I can keep this up."

"Y-you have to," said Bert, shivering. "I c-can't do it without you."

They carried on as the river steadily rose, covering their bound hands. Cam gasped for breath as it slapped against her belly.

"At least the water has f-frozen my wrists," she said. "I can hardly feel my lower half at all."

"Keep pulling," urged Bert. "The water will loosen the ro—"

He broke off as they were plunged into darkness. The flood had swallowed up their precious torch. Cam gave a little yelp.

"I'm all right," she gulped. "J-just keep working the rope – back, forward, back, forward – together."

"Don't lose hope, kids," called Gramps through the darkness. "There's always hope."

But the water had now engulfed their whole bodies.

"It's up to my neck," Cam whispered. "I can hardly move. S-somebody help us. HELP!"

"We're nearly there," said Bert. "I can feel it fraying."

Suddenly the rope snapped. The twins kicked their legs and wriggled free. They reached out for Gramps in the darkness. The water was covering his chin. They both dived down into the cold black water. Cam pulled desperately at the ropes that tied Gramps to the stalagmite. She could feel Bert tugging the other end. They came up a minute later gasping for air.

"There's nothing you can do for me," yelled Gramps. "Get out of here before the whole place fills to the roof. GO!"

"We're not leaving you," sobbed Cam, as Bert ducked down under the water again. "HELP! SOMEONE! ANYONE! HELP!"

Suddenly a familiar aroma began to fill the cavern. Bert resurfaced just as a loud splashing sound came from the narrow passage that led into the chamber.

"Someone's coming!" he panted. "HELP! HELP! DOWN HERE!"

A dark figure plunged into the cave. It was wearing a head torch so they couldn't see a face. It swam over to the leaking wall and stuffed something round into the hole, stopping the terrible sound of flowing water.

"I knew that lucky Stilton would come in handy one day," said Primula Mold.

# 24

## Rescue Mission
### (One hour to go. . .)

Primula Mold produced a knife from her pocket. She stuck it between her teeth, dived under and sliced through the rope. Gramps bobbed to the top of the water. She followed close behind and began swimming towards the narrow passage.

"Come on," she cried. "My lucky Stilton won't hold for long."

They followed her through the alley, which was now almost full to the ceiling. A gap of about thirty centimetres allowed them to breathe. Suddenly a loud POP sounded behind them, followed by a huge surge of water. They were propelled through the passage into the large cathedral cavern that lay beyond.

"The cheese has blown!" yelled Miss Mold. "The whole place is going to flood."

They waded through the rapidly filling cave to the other side. A pinhole of light shone through a tunnel at the far end.

"Hurry!" called Miss Mold.

They splashed through the tunnel, squinting against the light at the other end.

"It's morning already," cried Cam. "We've been in that cavern all night."

They emerged in a shallow cave. Fungus was waiting there. He ran around excitedly, his ears flapping against everyone's wet legs. At first Cam thought it was the same cave where Mr Zola had stored the moose cheese. But as she looked around her, she realized that they had come out in a different place.

"We'll be safe here," panted Miss Mold, leaning

against the wall and catching her breath. "The water won't get this far. Good boy for waiting, Fungus."

Gramps grabbed the twins and hugged them tightly against his chest. They all slowly sank to the floor.

"You saved their lives, Miss Mold," he said. "And mine too. How can we ever thank you?"

Miss Mold looked curiously at the three soggy people slumped on the ground like a heap of freshly caught fish. "You can start by telling me what on earth is going on," she said. "Fungus and I just came down to the cave to collect our moose cheese."

She pointed to a sparkling yellow cheese streaked with blue, tucked into a recess in the cave.

"I saw that Royal Cheesemaker fellow heading towards the State Banquet early this morning," she continued. "And I thought the twins would be close behind. So I rushed over here to grab my moose cheese. The Queen is bound to prefer mine. I've added a blue vein."

"Mouldy moose cheese," said Bert in awe. "Do

you think Mr Zola realized the caves were flooding when he came to pick up our moose cheese?"

"He couldn't have done," said Miss Mold. "It was very early when I saw him. The water wouldn't have reached the outer caves by then. But by the time I got here, I could hear the water rising. So I popped my head inside the cavern to have a quick look and heard someone scream. I got Fungus to guard the cheese and then ventured further in. I could hear you shouting for help."

"Thank you, Miss Mold," said Cam. "I thought you hated us."

"I don't hate you," cried Miss Mold. "And Fungus certainly doesn't. I just don't want you scaring my beloved goats with your constant fighting and screaming. My animals are very important to me."

Fungus gazed up adoringly at her as she tickled his chin.

"Sorry about that," said Bert. "We didn't mean to frighten your animals. But I thought you wanted to buy our land and bulldoze our farm."

"It's no secret that I want to extend my dairy,"

said Miss Mold. "And your land would come in very handy. But the truth is I would never demolish Whey Farm. It's a slice of cheese history. I was trying to wind up your Gramps so that he would enter the moose-cheese competition. We've been competing over the best cheese for more than fifty years. I was disappointed when he said he wasn't entering. It's not as much fun if I can't beat your grandfather – which I usually do."

"I beg to differ," said Gramps, getting to his feet. "You might have won best in show for the past few years, but before that—"

"Would you two stop arguing?" interrupted Bert. "It's so annoying listening to them bicker all the time, isn't it, Cam?"

Gramps and Miss Mold stared at him open-mouthed.

"Yes," agreed Cam. "You two need to stop fighting and work together. The Queen's life is at risk."

Miss Mold's eyes widened. "What do you mean?" she asked. "What's going on?"

Primula Mold listened attentively as the twins told her about Mr Zola's evil plan to poison the Queen.

"Rennet from the third stomach?" she gasped. "The villain! We must hurry. I saw the guests for the State Banquet arriving earlier. The Queen and Monsieur Grand-Fromage will be here anytime."

"Let's go!" yelled the twins.

"Are you ready, Mr Curd?" asked Miss Mold.

"Ready when you are, Primula," said Gramps. "And call me Cornelius."

# 25

## Time's Up!

The twins emerged from the cave, blinking in the bright sun with Gramps, Miss Mold and Fungus close behind. They scrambled up the steep path to the top of the gorge. It was very slippery from all the rain the night before. A huge purple marquee rose up in the distance with a red, white and blue helicopter hovering above it.

"That's her," shouted Gramps. "Quickly! The Queen has arrived."

They broke into a run. Gramps and Miss Mold lagged behind the twins with Fungus even further back, his short legs scrabbling frantically to keep up with everyone. They could hear the faint strains of "God Save the Queen" coming from a small orchestra, followed by "La Marseillaise".

"That's the French national anthem," puffed Gramps. "Monsieur Grand-Fromage has arrived too. Hurry!"

It was a warm day and the sides of the purple marquee had been taken down. Cam and Bert could see a long white table stretching the length of the marquee. Two large chairs were positioned in the centre. The gathered guests all got to their feet as the Queen came to the table. She was accompanied by a tall man with an extremely large nose.

"That must be Monsieur Grand-Nose," panted Bert. "I mean, Grand-Fromage."

As the twins got closer, a large soldier dressed in a scarlet jacket with a tall furry hat stepped in their path.

"Halt!" he said. "Only invited guests are allowed past this point."

"But the Queen is in terrible danger," cried Cam,

trying to barge her way past the soldier. He grabbed her arm, stopping her from going any further.

"Stop right there!" he yelled.

"Wait, you don't understand," shouted Bert. "She mustn't eat the moose cheese! Don't let her eat the cheese!"

"What are you talking about?" said the soldier, pulling out a walkie-talkie.

Bert tried to get by but the soldier grabbed him too.

"I have a disturbance on the south-west side," he barked into his radio. "Backup required."

Gramps and Primula Mold came puffing up, closely followed by two more soldiers.

"They're telling the truth," panted Gramps. "Let them go."

But the soldiers just stood in their way.

"Leave now," said one of them, "or I'll have you arrested for disturbing the peace."

Suddenly there was a loud cheer from the assembled guests. The twins peered round the soldiers to see Mr Zola approaching the table with a large silver platter covered with a shining domed lid. He bowed low before placing the platter in front of the Queen. The guests applauded enthusiastically.

"NO!" screamed Cam.

"STOP THAT MAN!" yelled Bert.

"That cheese is poisoned," said Gramps to one of the soldiers. "Your head will roll if you don't do something to stop this."

The soldier hesitated and looked at his colleagues.

"It's true!" screeched Primula Mold.

But the Queen was already taking the lid off. She smelled the large glowing cheese before accepting a sharp knife presented to her by a smiling Mr Zola. Monsieur Grand-Fromage also smelled the cheese. Cam thought she saw him frown as the Queen cut a small wedge.

"You have to stop this!" shouted Cam, trying to break free from the soldier. But he held them both firmly.

Out of the corner of her eye she saw Fungus come bounding up behind them. He jumped as high as his short legs allowed and nipped the soldier on the bottom. The soldier yelped and released Bert and Cam. The pair of them sprinted towards the banquet. They could hear the soldiers right behind them. Mr Zola's face fell as he saw them approaching.

"STOP!" screamed Cam.

"IT'S POISONOUS!" shouted Bert.

But it was too late. The twins watched in horror as the Queen lifted the wedge of deadly moose cheese to her mouth.

# 26

## The Moose Ranger

Cam and Bert continued to run towards the Queen but were rugby-tackled to the ground by the pursuing soldiers. From a crumpled heap, the twins watched as Monsieur Grand-Fromage leapt from his seat and knocked the wedge of moose cheese from the Queen's raised hand. The Queen shrieked (in a calm and regal way) as two of her bodyguards seized Monsieur Grand-Fromage. They in turn were seized by two of his bodyguards. Some of the guests started screaming. Mr Zola turned on his heels and began to walk away from the chaos.

*"Arret!"* shouted Monsieur Grand-Fromage. *"Ce fromage d'orignaux est toxique!"*

"I beg your pardon?" said the Queen.

"Those children are telling the truth," cried Monsieur Grand-Fromage. "This moose cheese is poisonous. I am a cheese connoisseur and I can smell the toxic rennet from here."

Two burly soldiers lifted the twins to their feet as Monsieur Grand-Fromage's bodyguards stepped away from the Queen's.

"Where is Mr Zola?" asked the Queen.

Mr Zola stopped mid-step. Monty was twitching nervously.

"Are these the children from Cheddar Gorge that you were telling me about?" she asked. "I thought you said they had disappeared and you couldn't find them."

"It's true, ma'am," said Mr Zola. "I now believe that they were in fact trying to poison you."

The Queen examined the stunned children and then turned to Mr Zola.

"If they were trying to poison me, Mr Zola,"

she said, "why would they then battle their way through my soldiers to inform me that the cheese was toxic?"

Mr Zola was silent and Monty began to droop. Gramps stepped up behind him and pulled the red pot of rennet with the skull and crossbones out of Mr Zola's pocket.

"Rennet from the third stomach of a Mongolian yak," said Gramps, holding it high for all to see. "Deadly – and added to the moose cheese by this man!"

There were gasps of shock and horror from the crowd as two soldiers grabbed Mr Zola. He pulled against them.

"I admit it's true!" he cried. "But the Queen was responsible for the death of my father. He died by moose and so shall she."

"Well, that's hardly likely any more, is it, Mr Zola?" said the Queen, calmly. "Thanks to these two children and Monsieur Grand-Fromage's prodigious nose for cheese."

She smiled and nodded to the twins and

Monsieur Grand-Fromage before turning back to Mr Zola.

"I remember your father well," she said. "He was a good man, and he would shudder to think you had turned to a life of crime."

"I am avenging his death!" shouted Mr Zola. "You forced him to make you moose cheese."

"I did nothing of the sort," retorted the Queen. "It was your father's lifelong dream to produce a moose cheese. It was his choice to attempt such a feat."

Mr Zola scowled. "You don't know how I've suffered," he muttered, madly. "I have been churned up like a milky mozzarella and it's your fault! I've fallen from the towers of St Basil's Cathedral, been threatened with arrest and nibbled by a crazed moose. I was whipped up by a whirlwind, plunged from a dam and rocketed through the sky in a deflating bouncy castle and . . . and . . ."

"Did I make you go on the Great Moose Cheese Chase, Mr Zola?" interrupted the Queen.

He looked at the ground and began to shuffle his feet.

"I seem to remember you volunteering," she continued. "In fact, I seem to remember you wholeheartedly supporting this competition."

Mr Zola continued to look at the floor, mumbling incoherently.

"You haven't answered my question, Mr Zola," said the Queen. "Did I force you to get involved in the moose cheese quest?"

"Erm . . . not exactly. . ."

"And I didn't ask your father to either," she said. "But he insisted on doing it. He was a brave man *and* a loyal member of staff, I might add."

Mr Zola continued shuffling. He wouldn't look at the Queen.

"Do you wish to apologize?" she asked.

"I think Monty does . . ." he murmured ". . . but I don't want to."

"Good, because it's too late for sorry. I hereby banish you to Siberia, where you will remain for the next five years, or until you have resolved your moose issues. I will speak with the Russian authorities and arrange a position for you as Moose Ranger."

"Moose Ranger?" shrieked Mr Zola. "B-but, Your Majesty, I can't do that. I'm moose-phobic. I had a terrible experience on the Trans-Siberian Railway."

"Well, it will allow you to face your fears, then," she said, "which is always a good thing. Now, take him away!"

The soldiers dragged Mr Zola into a waiting army van.

"What about Monty?" he cried, as they stuffed him into the back of the truck. "He had nothing to do with this. He's innocent! Don't punish him for my mistakes. . ."

The twins could still hear Mr Zola shouting as the heavy truck doors slammed shut.

"I almost feel sorry for him," whispered Cam as the van drove off.

"Well, don't," said Gramps. "We could have all died because of him."

"Besides," added Bert, "he'll be fine in Siberia. Remember how much that moose on the train liked him. I think he could become a moose whisperer."

They watched as the army van drove off into the distance. The excited chattering from the guests died down as the Queen got to her feet and prepared to address the crowd.

# The Queen's Speech

"Monsieur Grand-Fromage," said the Queen. "You have saved my life and so shall be awarded the Cheese Cross in honour of your sensitive nose and quick reactions."

Monsieur Grand-Fromage smiled and kissed the Queen's hand. "The honour is all mine, *Votre Majeste*," he said.

The Queen turned a regal shade of pink, then beckoned to Cam and Bert.

"Come forward," she commanded.

The twins stood in front of her.

"You fought against my very own soldiers to try and warn me of Mr Zola's treachery," she said. "And for this I award you. . ."

Bert held his breath. Was he going to become Lord Curd after all?

The Queen reached for a large bowl full of pastries. "I award you a cheese straw – one each."

Bert's face fell as she handed him a long thin pastry.

"I would also like to offer my patronage to your dairy farm," continued the Queen. "All your produce will now be 'by appointment to Her Majesty the Queen'."

She smiled and shook their hands, ending with a little push to show she had finished talking to them.

"What does that mean?" whispered Bert, slowly backing away.

"It means she'll buy her cheese from our farm," said Cam. "And because she will, so will lots of other people, because the Queen only buys the best. Look at Gramps' face."

The twins glanced over at a beaming Gramps. His

white whiskers were standing on end in excitement.

"That look is enough reward for me," whispered Cam.

"Me too," laughed Bert. "And with a royal stamp of approval, Whey Farm will be here for at least another four hundred years."

"Finally," continued the Queen, motioning for Primula Mold to step up, "the only contestant to actually produce a proper moose cheese."

Primula Mold stepped forward with Fungus at her heels.

"What a strange-looking corgi," said the Queen. "What's wrong with his ears?"

"He's a basset hound, ma'am," said Primula Mold, setting her moose cheese down on the table. "I have made a special moose cheese in honour of Your Majesty – I've added a blue vein."

The Queen raised her eyebrows as Monsieur Grand-Fromage inspected the cheese.

"I'm afraid that I asked for a traditional moose cheese," said the Queen. "Adding a blue vein is against the rules. So unfortunately, I cannot bestow a title or the prize money on you."

The smile on Primula Mold's face froze and Fungus began to howl.

"However," she continued, "I do like the odd bit of blue, especially Stilton, and Monsieur Grand-Fromage is very impressed."

He was already slicing into the cheese and smelling it with great gusto.

"I also appreciate the sentiment and the hard work that went into making it," she went on. "So, I'd be happy to offer your dairy my patronage too. I understand that both farms are close in proximity. It would be nice to see you working together. Maybe you could produce something even more precious than moose cheese. What do you say?"

Primula frowned as Fungus left her side and sat next to Gramps. He rested his head on Gramps' lap and looked up at his mistress with his enormous brown eyes.

"Don't you look at me like that, Fungus," she said. "You know I can't say no when you look at me like that. The problem is, I still need to extend my farm."

"You will," replied Gramps, rubbing the dog's head, "and so will I. Maybe it's time to join dairies and become that 'cheese force to be reckoned with' that we talked about all those years ago."

The frown between Primula's eyes slowly unfolded and her large eyes began to twinkle, lighting up her face.

"Maybe it is," she smiled. "That's if you can overcome your fear of mould spores."

"If mouldy cheese is good enough for the Queen, then it's good enough for me," said Gramps, grinning broadly. "How about . . . a Royal Blue Cheddar?"

"Fabulous!" cried the Queen. "Now, pull up a chair and let the banquet begin."

Dozens of serving staff jumped into action. Two cushioned chairs were produced for the twins and they sat opposite Monsieur Grand-Fromage. The mouldy moose cheese was sliced up and handed round to all the guests. The Queen took the first bite and nodded enthusiastically.

"It's marvellously moosey," she announced.

"Creamy but light, smooth, with a subtle crunch."

"That's the rock salt, ma'am," said Primula Mold. "I had to abseil down the deepest mine shaft to get that crystal."

"How I love to abseil," said the Queen. "Tell me, have you ever tried descending face down? Apparently one gets a splendid adrenalin rush. . ."

Monsieur Grand-Fromage leant over and offered the twins the last slice of moose cheese. The glow it emitted lit up their excited faces.

"You will have to share, I'm afraid," he said.

"*Merci*," said Cam, shyly.

"*Bon appetit*," he replied, before turning his attention back to the Queen.

"Are you ready for this?" asked Cam, holding up the slice.

"Yes!" cried Bert. "Mould or no mould – it's still moose cheese. I want to be healthy and wealthy."

But before Cam could break it in two, Fungus leapt up, grabbed it from her hand and dashed out of the marquee.

"Fungus, come back," called Miss Mold.

"We'll get him," said Bert.

The twins left their seats and ran down the hill after the lolloping dog. Bert caught hold of his collar just as he swallowed the last piece of cheese.

"Fungus! You greedy pooch!" cried Bert. "Now we're never going to find out what moose cheese tastes like."

Cam couldn't help giggling. "What a wild moose chase!" she laughed.

"We need to make another one!" said Bert. "But not just moose cheese. With your brains and my skill, we could make all kinds of exotic cheeses. Start a new business – *The Incredible Curd Twins' Incredible Cheese Things* – Elephant cheese, gerbil cheese, duck-billed platypus cheese!"

"Blue dog cheese?" asked Cam, patting Fungus.

Bert pulled a face and started laughing too. "Maybe not," he said. "But who knows! Anything is possible if you're an incredible Curd twin."

He put his arm around his sister, and together they walked back up the hill to have tea with the Queen.

# The End.